BUTTERMAKER TAUGHT THE BEARS EVERYTHING HE KNEW ABOUT BASEBALL. THE BEARS TAUGHT HIM EVERYTHING ELSE!

"PLAY BALL!" the umpire shouted, dusting off the plate and pulling on his mask.

Buttermaker hurriedly called his team together. "Boys, Amanda, I don't have to remind you what this game means to us. But I will anyway. It means we will be playing in the championship game against the Yankees. If we win. If we win. And what does that mean to the Athletics today? Ahmad, what does it mean?"

Ahmad flashed a wide, toothy grin. "It means a whole lot of BAAD NEWS for the ATHLET-ICS!"

"BAD NEWS for the ATHLETICS!" the team echoed together, as they burst out of the dugout to take the field.

THE BAD NEWS BEARS

Paramount Pictures Presents
A STANLEY R. JAFFE PRODUCTION
A MICHAEL RITCHIE FILM

WALTER MATTHAU
TATUM O'NEAL

THE BAD
NEWS BEARS

ALSO STARRING

VIC MORROW

Director of Photography
JOHN A. ALONZO, A.S.C.
Written by BILL LANCASTER
Produced by STANLEY R. JAFFE
Directed by MICHAEL RITCHIE
Music Adapted by JERRY FIELDING
In Color
A Paramount Picture

THE
BAD NEWS
BEARS

by Richard Woodley

based on the screenplay by
Bill Lancaster

A DELL BOOK

Published by
Dell Publishing Co., Inc.
1 Dag Hammarskjold Plaza
New York, New York 10017
Copyright © 1976 by Paramount Pictures Corporation
All rights reserved.

Dell ® TM 681510, Dell Publishing Co., Inc.
Printed in the United States of America
First printing—April 1976
Second printing—June 1976

THE
BAD NEWS
BEARS

CHAPTER 1

Morris Buttermaker sat in his battered old Cadillac taking swigs from a can of beer. He stared out at the small-scale baseball field. After a while, he looked down at the letter in his lap and read it again, for the third time:

Dear Mo,

I'm not angry anymore. I understand you better now than I did when you left. You want nothing for yourself, which is as sad as wanting everything, because you can never be satisfied either way. You avoid relationships with people—not just me, but everybody. You call that independence. But I think you are afraid. Afraid to admit that you need other people, and that other people might need you.

As a friend, somehow I still have hope for you. I wish you well in whatever you are doing these days.

Sincerely,
B.W.

Buttermaker stared blankly at the letter in his lap. In a way, he wished he hadn't received it. He didn't like to be analyzed. And he didn't like to be reminded of that happier time. Still, it was a contact with her, however slight. So he had read it each of the three mornings since receiving it, and now he had read it yet another time.

Then he sighed and leaned his head back. It bumped against various tools of his swimming-pool-cleaning business which were piled in the back seat. He rubbed his head. ". . . whatever you are doing these days." He chuckled at the irony of that. For what he was doing these days was involving himself with a whole bunch of little people he doubted he would understand at all.

He doubted he would understand them because he felt he didn't understand anybody very well—including himself half the time. He didn't even WANT to understand people, or be understood. He wanted to be left alone. Sort of. Since it seemed that whenever he got involved with anybody he ended up regretting it one way or another. And now, instead of being left alone, he was going to surround himself with a bunch of kids every day. How could you hope to understand kids if you didn't understand yourself?

He had been roped into this. He had been an easy mark for an appeal to his guilt, and payment of a few extra dollars—a pushover. Dollars he needed; pool-cleaning was providing him with a bare minimum for living. Guilt he had a surplus of, like anybody who hadn't bothered to donate to worthy causes or pay attention to social problems or vote for President. Or even raise a family of his own. That was the clincher. A man OWES something to kids—that was the reasoning he'd been given.

And so, since he didn't have any of his own to yell at,

the assumption was that he was obliged to give some of his time to other people's kids. Baloney. But for a few extra dollars . . .

He reached over to the glove compartment and took out a half-full bottle of Jim Beam whiskey. He poured a hefty slug of it into his beer can and drained the entire mix. He crumpled up the letter and tossed it onto the floor. Then he picked it up and put it, with the Jim Beam, in the glove compartment.

He gazed through the windshield, and the mid-morning sun beating on it caused him to squint. He pulled down the bill of his wrinkled black baseball cap to shade his eyes, and surveyed the field straight ahead, where a sprinkler turned lazily and cast a sheen over the outfield grass.

On the far fence, a sign reading NORTH VALLEY LEAGUE was being repainted by a workman. Nearby a father and son did jumping-jack exercises. A woman knelt in the dust of the base path and leaned over to hammer the second-base peg into the ground.

Suddenly Buttermaker was seized by a fit of coughing. He bent over in a choking spasm. He leaned against the car door and swung it open, the rust from its lower edge stirring in a brown mist above the parking-lot asphalt. He continued coughing as he stumbled out and across the field to the drinking fountain. Between hacks, he sipped from the mottled steel spout. And finally his body relaxed.

Buttermaker leaned on the fountain and closed his bloodshot eyes. He was thirty-five and felt fifty. His forehead was creased with a dozen furrows, and crow's-foot lines stretched away from his eyes. His cheeks were puffy, as was his nose, which showed the first signs of tiny, crosshatched red capillaries. His jaw was edged with jowls. Altogether, his face had a soft, lumpy look, the face of a man whose handsome lines had drooped, who didn't exercise his muscles often to laugh or smile. It was a tired face. Even his brown hair, cut short but not recently, curled wearily around his ears.

His body, though, was reasonably trim, with but a hint of paunch jutting atop his belt. His arms, sticking out from short, flowered sleeves, retained a lean hardness. His hands were large, square, sinewy. He flexed his fingers and made fists, habitually trying to loose the tightness which gripped them during periods of inactivity.

His legs, too, were strong and lean, though one wouldn't have guessed that, looking at the baggy chinos that draped loosely over them.

In time, Buttermaker opened his eyes a little and studied his feet, which were, in conformance with whatever he was doing these days, clad in worn sneakers. Lucky, he thought, given the price of shoes, that he could wear sneakers both for cleaning pools and for this.

He took a Tiparillo from his shirt pocket and squeezed the pockets of his pants for a lump that would be matches. He found none.

A flash exploded in his eyes, causing him to jump. It was a lighter, the wick adjusted like a torch, held to the tip of his slim cigar. Buttermaker said, "Thanks," before he glanced at the lighter's owner.

It was a boy, or the semblance of one. One of those who was stronger, taller, wiser than his age. His dark hair curled long over his ears and down the back of his neck. His eyes were sullen; he didn't smile or nod. He replaced the lighter in the watch pocket of his tight Levi's, which were tucked into knee-high motorcycle-racing boots with heavy buckles.

"Thanks again," Buttermaker said, looking at him now.

The boy said nothing, turned, and walked away over to a small Harley-Davidson left cocked on its stand. It was black, except for heavy streaks of chrome. Mirrors adorned both handlebars. The boy quickly slung himself astride it, kicked over the engine, leaned back against the tall chrome backrest, roared into a dust-spewing wheelie, and disappeared through the parking lot and away on the road.

Buttermaker watched him leave, absently dusting himself off even though no dust had reached him, and took his first drag on the Tiparillo. The coughing returned, and he doubled over.

"Buttermaker, where in blazes you been, what kept you?"

He straightened up to see, running over to him, a familiar man of about his age, wearing tennis shorts and sweater, deeply tanned, clean-shaven, blond, combed, sinewy as a colt.

"Hi, Whitewood. Had a pool to clean." Buttermaker coughed some more.

"I don't think you've met my boy, Toby." Whitewood produced from behind him an eleven-year-old, dressed in cutoff jeans and sneakers, as tanned as his father, but with longer blond hair down to his shoulders. "He'll be playing for you."

"Hi, Coach," Toby said.

Buttermaker fluttered a hand limply in greeting.

Whitewood clapped his hand on Buttermaker's back, bringing forth a few more coughs. "I really appreciate this, old pal," he said. "It's just a darn shame that none of the fathers had the time for it. God knows, I'd be coaching them myself if I wasn't so gosh-awful busy down at City Hall . . ."

Buttermaker was listlessly staring at the rear of the woman hunched over second base. Without turning his face, he said, "Got my check, Bob?"

Whitewood quickly shoved his son behind him and motioned him away. He took Buttermaker by the elbow and steered him toward the pitcher's mound. He glanced around nervously. "Isn't that supposed to be just between you and me?" he asked, a touch of irritation in his voice.

"Yeah, sorry."

Whitewood put a folded envelope into Buttermaker's hand. "So let's keep it that way, hunh?"

Buttermaker pocketed the envelope and blinked hard twice, leaning his head back and rolling it around his shoulders. Whitewood bounced lightly on the balls of his feet and glanced into the dugout. "It's gonna be tough," he said, "since we got into this so late. Jiminy, one week to opening day."

Buttermaker had returned his attention to the woman installing the base. Whitewood smiled and put a hand on his shoulder. "The only game played around here," he said with a wink, "is baseball, chum."

Buttermaker nodded. "Sure, right."

Whitewood glanced at his gold watch and bounced on his toes. "Wanted to introduce you to some of the administrators and players around here, but I'm running late."

"Aren't we all," said Buttermaker, smiling.

"Hunh?"

"Nothing."

Whitewood took a sheet of paper from his hip pocket, unfolded it, and handed it to Buttermaker. "Here's a list of the boys' names. To get you oriented and supplied, ask for the woman they call Pigtails. She'll get you all set. And don't let any of these kids give you a hard time. You're the boss, Coach." He looked around quickly, then leaned in to Buttermaker's ear confidentially. "Just to grease the skids a little, I already told the kids something about your career, embellished it a little, you know. I even mentioned that you once taught that little Amanda how to throw a curve ball."

Buttermaker closed his eyes.

Whitewood turned slowly to scan the nearly empty field. He smiled and nodded. "I think we're doing a really fine thing," he said in ministerial tones, "I really do."

Buttermaker extracted the envelope from his pocket, opened it, took out the check, looked at it briefly, and said, "Yeah."

Whitewood waved briskly and trotted off toward the parking lot, from which his son was now returning on his ten-speed bicycle.

Buttermaker walked slowly toward the woman, who had now moved over to third and was trying to pound the bag into place. Whitewood's son, Toby, followed, pedaling easily.

"You played with Dad in high school, hunh?"

"Yeah," said Buttermaker gruffly, without looking back.

"He says you were really great once."

"Nice of him."

"Is it true that you once taught a nine-year-old girl how to throw a curve?"

"Yes."

A man bellowed at Toby from the dugout: "GET THAT DARN THING OFF THE INFIELD!"

The sudden outburst caused Toby to lose control and almost fall over. He quickly righted himself, clanked the bike into the proper gear, finally picked up speed, and raced off the field, hunched over with his head down.

Buttermaker turned toward the source of the yell, coughed once, tapped the ashes off his cigar, clamped it back between his teeth, and walked up to third base.

The woman tipped her head up to smile at him. She was pretty, even though sweat streaked her face, her long brown hair hung in tangles, and her jeans and shirt were smeared with dirt. Buttermaker smiled back.

She sighed and returned to her work. "Sorry he yelled at your boy like that," she said between grunts as she wrestled with the base. "My husband's got this passion over the condition of the infield."

"It's not my boy," Buttermaker said. "My name's Buttermaker. Are you Pigtails?"

"Hardly," she said, briskly shaking her head and chuckling. She looked up at him. "Hardly. I think she's inside, in the snack bar, messing with the equipment. Buttermaker? The new coach?"

"No less."

"Well." She stood up, dusted off her hands on her jeans, and stuck out her right one. "Welcome aboard. I'm Jill Turner. My husband, Roy, is the loudmouth." She smiled as they shook hands. "Good luck."

"Thanks," he said, rubbing the back of his neck and rolling his head around. Then he looked up at her with mock sternness, jabbing the air with his finger. "We'll drive 'em till their legs buckle, practice 'em till their heads ache, knock spirit into 'em, and mold 'em into winners, or my name ain't—"

"Buttermaker," she said. "That's an unusual name."

"Grandma loved the dairy business," he said.

Jill laughed, squinting into the sun and wiping sweat off her forehead with her arm. "You sound just like my husband, with all that drive-knock-winners stuff."

14

"Glad to hear there's another competitive soul around here."

"Oh, he's competitive, all right. Nothing but champions for us."

"I guess I better check in with Pigtails," he said. "See you later."

"Good."

Buttermaker strolled over to the snack bar and tried the front gate, which was locked, then went around to the back and pushed open the creaky wooden door.

Something swatted the wall beside his head. He ducked.

"Sorry." A woman of formidable dimension and voice came around the counter toward him. "Catcher's mask got away from me." She retrieved the mask, which had narrowly missed Buttermaker, and tossed it on top of the counter, adding it to a mountain of small-size baseball gear.

She returned to her task of sorting and piling, occasionally hurling some piece of faulty equipment away against a wall. Her pigtails swung around her busy head, upon which was perched a baseball cap stuck full of pins of past league champions. An unlit cigarette dangled between her lips.

Buttermaker approached cautiously. "You must be—"

"Pigtails," she said firmly, turning to look at him and placing her large hands on her wide hips and arching her mammoth chest against a tight-fitting jersey across which was stenciled CLEVELAND—CHAMPS '54.

"I'm Pigtails. What're you staring at?"

"Cleveland," he said, trying a smile.

"Read it and weep," she said. "Who're you?"

"Buttermaker. Morris Buttermaker. I'm the new—"

"Christmas if you ain't. Yeah. New coach of the new

team. The Bears. That'll take some getting used to. Yeah. Crazy lawsuits are gonna be the ruin of this country. No offense, of course. That's old Whitewood's doing. This here's your pile." She shoved a duffle bag at him. "Load up, and no complaints. We weren't expecting this. You take what's left."

"It's okay." He began jamming the gear into the duffle bag.

Pigtails softened her tone a bit. "Wasn't so bad when the courts made us take in the girls, because the ones who came out could cut it. But now this." She thumped her fist on the counter. "Nothing personal, of course. But Lord awmighty! Since when is it a court's business to tell us how many teams we gotta have in this league?"

Buttermaker started to pack in the catcher's mask which had just earlier dented the wall beside his head. Then he took it back out and held it up. Half the pad inside the bars was missing, and one strap was broken. "I guess this has kind of had it," he said.

"Now YOU got it, Buttermaker," Pigtails said, "and see to it that it lasts all fifteen games. This is the best I could do. You're lucky there's anything, what with—"

"Give the guy a break, Pigtails."

Buttermaker turned to see Jill Turner standing in the open doorway, smiling broadly.

"None of this is his fault," she said. "He's just here to help the boys."

Pigtails grunted.

A large man, dark-haired, broad-shouldered, heavy-chested, big-bellied, pushed his way in past Jill. "See, Buttermaker," the man said, "the problem here is that your friend Whitewood could have gotten his son and the rest of those boys into hundreds of other leagues around Los Angeles. We're different from other leagues around here, especially in the Hollywood area. Some of them don't care about the level of play. But we run a highly competitive program. It's the boys themselves who want it that way."

He stuck out his hand, as an afterthought. "Hi, I'm Roy Turner."

Buttermaker met his grip, and winced. "Strong hand, Roy."

"Oh yeah, sorry, I always forget."

Buttermaker snickered. "Seem's like EVERY-BODY'S sorry since I got here."

"Naw, naw, glad to have you," Turner said. "It's just that we have this problem." He leaned back against the counter and folded his arms and narrowed his eyes. "See, Buttermaker, all we want here is the very best program for the boys. And what the boys want is the very best brand of baseball they can play. If you can fit your, uh, team into that, then everybody'll be happy."

"Sounds just great," Buttermaker said, slinging the duffle bag over his shoulder.

"Heard you were once a pretty good ballplayer yourself," Turner said, looking him up and down.

"Fair, a long time ago."

"Not so long, Buttermaker, couldn'ta been too long ago. I once played a decent brand myself. Maybe you'd like to fling a few sometime."

"Well, I doubt I could—"

"It's a date, Buttermaker."

"Yeah, well, I got to get out and round up my boys."

"Good luck," the other three said in unison.

Buttermaker started out the door, then stopped. "By the way, who was that . . ." He started to ask about the boy on the motorcycle, then thought better of it. "Uh, see you all on the field of play, as they say in show biz."

He pulled the door shut behind him and sighed deeply as he trudged away toward the diamond.

Morris Buttermaker felt like a very old man as he stood puffing his Tiparillo before the group of small boys who were dressed in an assortment of jeans or shorts, sneakers, T-shirts, and various colors of baseball caps.

They were smaller than he had expected. "Pipsqueaks" was a word that popped into his mind. But in truth he didn't know whether they were big or small for their age. How old were they? Nine? Thirteen? Eleven? He hadn't taken the time to brush up on requirements for the Bears. He just knew that they were boys.

Beyond that, his initial brief assessment was that they didn't look like a team of anything at all. No two looked alike, dressed alike, or stood alike. They had long hair and short, black hair and blond, light complexions and dark. A couple wore glasses, which caught the sun and reflected it annoyingly into Buttermaker's ravaged eyes.

Somehow this would become a team, his team. As soon as he got them on the field, he thought, they would look like a team.

He held a sheet of paper in front of him and nodded to them. They nodded back, and fidgeted with their hands and feet. "Well, I'm Morris Buttermaker, your coach, as I guess you figured out. And you're the Bears, which I figured out all by myself."

He smiled and waited for laughter. There was none. He cleared his throat. "We haven't got much time before the season starts, just a week, so we'll have to get organized in a hurry. When I read off your names, step forward and tell me what positions you want to play."

"What positions ARE there?" came a voice from the group.

Buttermaker scanned the group quickly and coughed. A titter came from the nearby stands. Buttermaker was mildly annoyed to see several onlookers seated there, including a few boys, the Turners, Pigtails, and a handful of other adults. He cleared his throat. "Okay . . ." He traced his finger under a name and blinked to clear his watering eyes. "Lefty Stein?"

Lefty Stein stepped forward and stood ramrod straight, as if at attention. He was tall, all skin and bones, a stringbean, with a shock of black hair sticking down under the bill of his cap and almost reaching his eyes. He was wearing baseball pants a couple of sizes too short. "Here, Coach. Pitcher and shortstop."

"Short?" Buttermaker said, blinking.

"Yes, sir. You can't pitch every game, so—"

"Okay, okay."

An adult couple, Latin-complexioned, both dressed as if for church but with clothing too heavy for the season, had been slowly approaching from the stands, a couple of steps at a time, the man moving only when prodded by the woman. They stood now directly behind Buttermaker, who was startled by a tap on his arm.

"Excuse," the man said. "My name Luis Agilar." The man stood a full head shorter than Buttermaker, who was an even six feet, and looked straight at the coach's neck. He held a piece of paper, and adjusted his glasses. "My wife, Maria Agilar"—he gestured grandly at the woman—"and my two son, Miguel an' Jose." He waved a hand similarly at the two small, dark boys, who promptly stepped forward. Mrs. Agilar blushed and looked at the ground, and the boys copied her.

Mr. Agilar held the paper high and said quietly, "I

19

write to make easy, because the words I forget too soon."

Buttermaker shoved his cap back and squeezed his forehead with his hand and shut his eyes. "Yes?"

Mr. Agilar cleared his throat and read hesitatingly. "We been to America only one . . . month. My two boy speak a little the English, but learn at the school . . ."

An obese boy had waddled up from the parking lot, and now stood beside Buttermaker, looking him over, while munching the last of a peanut-butter sandwich.

Mr. Agilar went on: "We are family that love the baseball. In our homeland, Santo Domingo, the baseball is very . . . popoolar . . ."

"You Buttermaker?"

Buttermaker glanced down at the round boy and nodded, then turned back to Mr. Agilar.

". . . At first they say the boy are no good and can no play in this, um . . ."

"League?" Buttermaker suggested.

"League!" Mr. Agilar said, smiling broadly.

The round boy unwrapped a fresh sandwich, crinkling the aluminum wrap loudly. He took a mouthful. "I'm Engelberg," he said. "I'm on your team."

Buttermaker nodded and put a finger to his lips.

Mr. Agilar was oblivious to the interruption, and continued. "But then one day Mr. Whitewood call and say my two boy can play in the little baseball, on a new team just form NOW!" He beamed and looked up at Buttermaker.

"Did you really pitch for the Yankees?"

"Hey, Engelberg." Buttermaker grasped the boy's shoulder firmly. "Cool it."

"My wife"—Mr. Agilar again motioned to his blushing mate—"she think Mr. Whitewood is maybe saint. I no sure abou' that. But a good man, yes, for SURE!"

"My Dad's been a Yankee fan all his life—"

"Shut up, Engleberg!" came from the group.

"—and he said he never heard of no Buttermaker that ever played for the Yankees, let alone one that pitched a no-hitter."

Buttermaker turned Engleberg around by the shoulders and propelled him into the group, while Mr. Agilar put away his paper and glasses and smiled. He stuck out his hand to shake with Buttermaker.

"You've very welcome here," Buttermaker said. He turned to face the boys.

"Guys, listen. Let's get one thing straight. It's true I was a good ballplayer in my day, but I never played for the Yankees. As a matter of fact—"

"As a matter of fact, you never played in the major leagues." A small, bespectacled boy with straight blond hair parted near the middle stood with an index finger raised and looked straight ahead, not directly at Buttermaker, but into the distance. He wheezed and continued: "But you did pitch for Phoenix of the Pacific Coast League . . ."

Buttermaker stood with his mouth open, starting to speak. Then he relaxed and folded his arms.

"My research shows," the boy went on, stopping occasionally to wheeze, "that in 1965 you won nine games and lost six. With 117 strikeouts, 46 bases-on-balls, and an earned-run average of 2.86."

The rest of the boys shifted their feet nervously; a couple muttered.

"In 1966, however, you had a relatively disappointing season, winning only four games while losing fifteen—"

"My friend," Buttermaker interrupted, "whoever you are, how did you know all that—which is accurate, by the way—all that history of yours truly?"

"That's Ogilvie," said a neatly dressed boy politely. "He knows everything."

"Except," said Engelberg, his mouth full of something, "normal things like how to see straight and how to breathe."

"I will ignore that last comment," said Ogilvie, waving a finger at Engelberg. He took a quick sniff from a small tube of asthma-medication spray, then turned back to Buttermaker and adjusted his glasses. "More specifically, Coach Buttermaker, I have attempted to commit to memory the names and respective records of every person who ever played major-league baseball from 1871 to the present."

Buttermaker tilted his head back and studied the sky.

"And since I had never heard of you, prior to the formation of this team, I gathered that your playing career might have been exaggerated." He smiled confidently, and took the opportunity to wheeze. "So I went to the sports department of the newspaper and checked through their files. That's how I found out that you played in the minors for Phoenix. Further—"

"That's enough." Buttermaker spread his arms before him to still all the talk and muttering. "Good work, uh, Ogilvie. Now then, you other players." He looked back at his sheet. "Ahmad Abdul, uh, Rahim," he said. "I hope I pronounced that correctly."

"Yes, sir!" A compact, sinewy black boy with a neatly combed afro, wearing a T-shirt on which had been crudely scrawled the number *44,* stepped forward and saluted. "I like to play where Hank Aaron did, also swish-hit like my big brothers."

"Aaron played right field," Ogilvie said, his finger raised.

"Right field then."

"Also," Ogilvie added, "in his later years Aaron saw

22

a lot of action at first base, a position to which many older outfielders move when their legs have slowed."

"Then first base too."

"And, interesting to note," continued Ogilvie, as Buttermaker took a deep breath and closed his eyes, "is the little-known fact that Aaron also played a few games at second base, in 1955, 1960, 1964—"

"Okay, OKAY!" Buttermaker said.

"Then second base too, Coach. Everywhere Hank Aaron played."

"All right, all right. Mike Engelberg?"

"My dad thinks I should try out for catcher."

"He's got the right idea," Buttermaker said, suppressing a smile.

"What's that supposed to mean?" Engelberg asked defensively, ceasing his chewing.

"Uh, just that catchers are traditionally sturdy, strong types, like Johnny Bench or Yogi—"

"Engelberg's really valuable," said Toby Whitewood, a hand over his mouth, " 'cause he can cover the plate and third at the same time."

Several boys giggled.

"Just keep it up, Whitewood," Engelberg said, flashing a fat fist holding two marshmallows, "if you want to get kung-fu'd!"

Several boys immediately squared off in karate positions, and split the air with mock chops and yelps and squeaks.

"Geez!" Engelberg said indignantly.

The boys continued leaping and swinging and yelping.

"TIMMY LUPUS!" hollered Buttermaker. The noise around him stopped abruptly. "Uh, Timmy Lupus?"

No one spoke. Boys looked at the ground.

"Lupus?" Buttermaker looked at them. Slowly a few heads turned to face one delicate, rather pale boy, who was standing a bit apart from them, staring at his shoes. He slowly patrolled his left nostril with his index finger.

"Geez, that Lupus makes me want to puke" came a whisper from a short, wiry, ruddy-faced redhead with a scab on his chin and a welt under his eye.

"Lupus?"

Timmy Lupus cautiously raised his hand.

"Ah, there you are. What position?"

"I . . . uh," he said weakly.

"He's shy, Coach," said the neatly dressed boy who had spoken up earlier for Ogilvie, "that's all."

"Shy my armpit," said the boy with the battered face, "he's just dumb."

"Shut up, Tanner," said the neat boy, to whom Buttermaker took an instant liking. "He's just kind of quiet, Coach."

"Since neither of you two arguers is quiet, why don't you give me your names?"

"I'm Jimmy Feldman, Coach," said the neat one. Buttermaker realized that one reason he liked him so quickly was that he looked at least a bit like an athlete, taller than most, willowy, with broad shoulders. But unfortunately he was also one of those wearing glasses, so that every time Buttermaker looked at him, he was forced to blink at the sun's reflection. "I'll play outfield, or wherever you need me. And that's Tanner Boyle."

"I'll run my own show, Feldman," Tanner said. "I'm Tanner Boyle. I'll handle short."

"Fine," Buttermaker said. He liked that boy too, a little. Tanner was not tall, but was obviously strong, the muscles already rippling on his young arms. He stood with legs planted apart defiantly. His dark hair was long and straight, but hung unevenly, as if cut at home. "Now, Timmy Lupus?"

Timmy, stung by having caused a minor rumpus, had retreated more. He hung his head.

"If you ask me," said Ogilvie, raising his finger, "I think Timmy and I would do a fine job sharing—"

"PITCHER!" Timmy Lupus barked suddenly, then slunk behind the crowd of boys as several tittered.

"I was about to say," Ogilvie said, "that Timmy and I could alternate in right field, which is generally considered the least demanding position. Though I emphasize, only on certain occasions, such as in the late innings, when we're behind by perhaps ten runs or more."

"Let's not start by putting ourselves down, boys," Buttermaker said in fatherly tones. "Let's see, who's left? Toby Whitewood I have already met."

"Outfield," Toby said, "probably center, 'cause I'm kinda fast."

"And 'cause your father," Tanner spat, "kinda owns the team."

"Knock off that garbage, Tanner," Buttermaker said. "I run this team. Nobody owns it. Regi Tower?"

Regi raised his hand, and Buttermaker recognized him as the boy who had been doing jumping jacks with his father when he arrived. Regi, a soft, fleshy boy with light, curly blond hair, turned to glance at his father in the stands. "Well, I'm supposed to try third," he said softly, not looking at Buttermaker.

"The hot corner, good. Now, the Agilar boys, Jose and Miguel?"

The two boys stepped forward soberly.

"Positions?"

They looked at each other.

"Okay," Buttermaker said, closing his eyes and tucking his roster into his shirt pocket. "Enough of this.

Let's see how we handle ground balls. Take the field, Bears."

The Bears, finally released from uncomfortable quizzing, leaped into action, bumping into one another, stumbling, cursing, and dispersing over the diamond.

Buttermaker tossed the duffle bag next to home plate and took out a bat and ball. A woman a bit younger than he, neat and primly clutching her purse, called to him from behind the backstop. "Mr. Buttermaker?"

He turned. "Yes?"

Her face, though young, was lined and serious. Buttermaker walked back to the screen, flipping the ball in one hand. "Yes?"

"I'm Mrs. Lupus," she said, in a voice so soft that Buttermaker was forced to lean against the screen to hear, "Timmy's mother."

"Uh-HUNH."

"I just wanted to tell you that, well, I want Timmy to play and all, but, just, uh . . ."

"You can speak frankly to me, Mrs. Lupus."

"Thank you. I just wanted to say that Timmy's kind of different, you know . . ."

"How different?"

"Well, he's kind of a, uh, slow learner, if you know what I mean, and . . ."

"Hey, I was slow as a kid too, Mrs. Lupus. There should be no problem—"

"Please, Mr. Buttermaker, try to understand. I don't want Timmy treated any differently from the other boys, or for you to spend more time working with him or anything. I only want to make you aware that you'll have to be, uh, patient."

Meanwhile, the boys on the field were being taunted by a bigger boy and his friends in the stands. "Hey,

Bears, what color are your uniforms going to be? Pink or something?" The boy and his friends guffawed.

"Come out here and say that, Turner!" yelled Tanner Boyle.

"Lucky for you I don't."

"Oh YEAH?"

"YEAH!"

Buttermaker surveyed the scene, then smiled at Mrs. Lupus. "Patience, Timmy's mother, is a requirement in any case. Timmy will be fine."

Mrs. Lupus smiled shyly, thanked him, and walked briskly away.

Glancing into the stands behind her, Buttermaker saw Mr. Agilar reading from his paper to Roy Turner and Pigtails. He sighed and strode to the plate.

The Bears were spread randomly around the infield, pounding fists into their gloves. Behind Buttermaker crouched Engelberg, chomping noisily on a candy bar.

"Engelberg," said Buttermaker, "can you hold off on the eating until after practice?"

"There's energy in chocolate. I need the energy."

Buttermaker took a deep breath and cocked the bat over his shoulder. "All right, Bears," he yelled to the team, "get one!"

He tapped a slow roller toward Lefty Stein, near third base. Lefty crouched carefully, watching the ball slither across the grass. But the ball slipped under his glove, ricocheted off his ankle and bounced up to hit his knee, rolled away, and stopped. Lefty pounced on it, stumbled, picked it up, and threw it in the direction of first base as he fell on his face.

The ball bounced four times enroute toward first, eluded Ahmad Abdul Rahim, who was covering, hopped to the fence, and rebounded into right field.

Timmy Lupus scurried over toward it, but overran it,

stepped on it, and fell on his rump. He got up quickly
and grabbed it and threw with a loud grunt toward Buttermaker. But the ball looped only fifteen feet, which
meant that it reached Ogilvie, who was also standing in
right. Ogilvie, in the process of spraying asthma medication into his nose, jumped with surprise when the ball
trickled across his foot. He picked it up and rolled it
back to Buttermaker.

In the stands, Roy Turner's son, Joey, and his pals
screeched with laughter and pounded one another. Roy
Turner and Pigtails exchanged shakes of their heads.

The Bears were embarrassed. Tanner Boyle kicked
up a cloud of baseline dirt. Timmy Lupus faced the
right-field fence. Lefty Stein, who had started it all, remained on his knees, staring at the ground.

Buttermaker disregarded the play. "Come on, get
one!" He hit another grounder at Regi Tower, between
third and short. Regi stumbled backward to avoid the
ball, and it dribbled past him to come to rest on the
left-field grass.

"Regi, blast you!" came the voice of his father from
the stands. "I told you to ATTACK that ball!"

Regi nodded sheepishly, took the short throw in from
Tanner, and rolled it underhand in to Engelberg, who
handed it to Buttermaker.

"All right, let's go, get . . ." Buttermaker looked
down at the ball in his hand. It was smeared with chocolate.

"Engelberg."

"What?"

"Look at the ball."

"Yeah?"

"Well, don't you see it's got CHOCOLATE all over
it? Didn't I ask you to put that away?"

Engelberg slammed his mitt to the ground. "Look,

Mr. Buttermaker," he whined, "quit bugging me about my food. People are always bugging me about it. My shrink bugs me about it. Now my coach bugs me about it—"

"I'm not trying to—"

"So you're not doing me any good. A boy of my size needs more food. So just quit bugging me."

Buttermaker pursed his lips. "Okay." He wiped the ball off on his pants. "Okay, look alive now, Bears. Get one!" This time he tapped out a short bunt which rolled to a stop a few feet in front of the plate. Nobody moved.

"Engelberg."

"What?"

"That's a bunt. That's the catcher's ball."

"It's got chocolate all over it."

"Oh, for PETE'S SAKE!" Buttermaker stomped his foot. "Field the bunt and throw to first base!"

Engelberg took off his mask and waddled out to the ball, muttering under his breath. "You were always yelling out to THEM, how was I supposed to know it was for ME?"

Engelberg threw accurately to first base, but unfortunately caught Ahmad looking into the stands. The ball bounced off his shoulder and landed on the bag. Ahmad snatched it up triumphantly. "OUT!" he cried.

Buttermaker rubbed his temples and coughed. "Good throw, Engelberg. Wake up out there! Here's another one!"

Buttermaker bunted again, and Engelberg leaped out to field it, whirled, and heaved the ball high over first, high over right field, and into the windshield of Buttermaker's Cadillac.

The smash of glass froze the action on the field. Everybody stared at the car.

29

Engelberg stuck out his lower lip in a pout. "Don't blame me. I didn't even know it was your car. A good first-baseman would've stretched—"

"Forget it," Buttermaker said. "Everybody stay right where you are," he called out. "I'll be right back."

Buttermaker figured he should care about the windshield, but in truth he didn't—not much. It was just another minor blow in a day of minor blows, like all his days in recent memory. And this gave him a chance to visit his car, which he had been wanting to do for the last half-hour. He needed a little pickup.

He slid into the front seat and looked through the windshield. Through the spiderweb of smashed safety glass, the Bears looked like scattered pieces of unrecognizable people, which was an accurate picture of the way he saw them.

There was nothing in them, or certainly in the way they played baseball, that he recognized. He was depressed. The longer he sat, the more depressed he got. It dawned on him only gradually just how bad they were. Those first few minutes of practice, which had passed too quickly for him to absorb, now lay in the pit of his stomach in a concentrated lump of depression.

What had he expected? They were just boys, after all. No, it was worse than that. They were worse than just a bunch of boy baseball players. So much of his life had been spent playing baseball, from his earliest years. One thing he knew was baseball, and every fiber of his body was attuned to what was good and what was bad, what was talent and what was not. So his very bones ached with the one thing he did recognize: He had a lousy team to coach.

But maybe not. They had practiced only a few minutes, after all. He snapped open a can of beer and drank a big gulp. Then he took out the Jim Beam, added it to refill the can, and got out of the car, taking the can with him.

Maybe they had just been nervous, this being their first practice with him. He leaned against the fender and took a long drink. He felt better instantly, even as he was walking back to the field. They couldn't be that bad.

"All right, Bears," he called, waving his arm, "bring it in."

The Bears gathered around him at home plate, eyeing the beer can, which he swished from side to side. Buttermaker felt goodwill surging through him. "Don't worry about the car, boys. I wanted a new windshield anyway. The old one was dirty." He smiled, but nobody laughed. He cleared his throat. "Now, have any of you boys ever played baseball before?"

"Hey, wait a minute." Tanner Boyle elbowed his way through his teammates to stand toe-to-toe with Buttermaker. He stared through narrowed eyes at the beer can, then slowly ran his gaze up to Buttermaker's face, which beamed down at him benevolently. Tanner jutted out his jaw and clenched his fists. "We miss a few ground balls," he hissed, "and right away you figure we never played before, HUNH? Well, that ain't the kind of talk I like, not from ANYBODY!"

He took a step back and put up his fists, an honorable David confronting a stunned Goliath.

Buttermaker stammered, "I, uh, um, why, um, uh . . ."

Jimmy Feldman jumped forward and clasped his arms around Tanner from the rear. "Come on, Tanner, you been in enough fights already this week."

Tanner struggled a little. Jimmy held on.

"Que pasa?" Miguel Agilar said to his brother.

"Como se yo?" Jose said, holding out his palms.

"Come on, Tanner," Jimmy said, still holding him,

"we're supposed to be a team, and the poor Agilar boys don't even understand what's going on."

"Aw, you feel sorry for everybody," Tanner said, beginning to relax.

Lefty Stein had been eyeing the stands, where Joey Turner and his bunch were doubled up with laughter. "Makes me sick," he said, "all those guys laughing at us."

Tanner broke free from Jimmy's grasp and whirled on Lefty, his fists jammed straight down, his face contorted in rage. "Well, what do you EXPECT!" he yelled. "All we got on this team is a bunch of JERKS, FOREIGNERS, SISSIES, and"—he hooked a thumb wickedly at Timmy Lupus—"NOSE-PICKING MORONS!"

Tanner spat on the ground, folded his arms, and faced away from the team.

"Tanner," Ogilvie said calmly, "I think you should be reminded from time to time that you are one of the few people on this team who HAS played baseball before, and one of the few who is NOT, as you so crudely put it, a jerk, foreigner, sissy, or moron." He walked around to Tanner's front and raised a finger in his face. "And so you'd better calm down, or the rest of us might be disposed to REMOVE you."

"Oh YEAH?" Tanner said, striking a boxer's pose.

Buttermaker quickly walked among the boys, separating them all with gentle shoves. "Gentlemen," he said, "let's return to the field of play."

The Bears were relieved to sprint back out to the diamond.

CHAPTER 2

Buttermaker stared at the banner hanging above the door of the Pizza Hut, billowing in the warm breeze under the floodlight. The banner read: WELCOME NORTH VALLEY LEAGUE.

He leaned against the hood of his car until he finished his Tiparillo, the final embers of which glowed in the evening darkness. And then, unable to delay longer, he squared his shoulders and went in.

On a table in the center of the room was a huge pizza designed to look like a baseball field. Green peppers were the outfield grass, pepperoni the infield dirt, mushrooms the bases, and a heap of anchovies the pitcher's mound.

Milling around the table and about the room was a throng of adults, most of whom were parents of boys in the league. Wives bunched with wives; fathers talked baseball with fathers.

"Boy, that little Carl Karansky sure has grown, gonna hit a ton this year."

"Should be playing Pony League."

"Whatever happened to little Eddie Wakely after he hit .725?"

"Went to college, I think, Santa Barbara or Santa something."

"I guess it'll be the Yankees again this year, hunh?"

"Well, things will be a little strange. That darned seventh team will sure screw up—"

The last speaker, Roy Turner, halted his sentence upon seeing Buttermaker brush by.

Most of the fathers were wearing jackets and ties. Buttermaker had on a pullover sweater. He pushed through, nodding occasionally to a parent who recognized him, and sat down at a table with Pigtails and Jill Turner.

"Hi," Jill said.

He nodded and reached immediately for the pitcher of beer.

"Glad you could make it, Buttermaker," Pigtails said. She had an evening dress deployed over her ample body, and her baseball cap was pinned to the back of her head.

"Wouldn't have missed it for the world," Buttermaker said, pouring himself a mugful and topping off the mugs of Jill and Pigtails.

Pigtails quaffed half a mug and licked her lips. "We have one of these every year. It's good to get things off on a friendly note."

"I'm afraid Morris hasn't been treated in a very friendly way so far," Jill said, touching his arm and smiling.

Buttermaker waved a denial with his hand.

"Well, sometimes we don't all get along too well AFTER the season starts," Pigtails said. "How are your uniforms coming along?"

34

Buttermaker wrinkled his brow. "Uniforms?"

"Better get on the ball with that," Pigtails said. "Bunch of colors are already taken—blue, green, red . . ."

"The Yankees have red," Jill said. "What will yours be?"

Buttermaker looked from Jill's face to Pigtails's. "I'm afraid we're a little behind." He got up. "Excuse me."

He elbowed his way over to the bar, where Whitewood was explaining a recent City Council vote.

". . . But if I hadn't sided with the Republicans, we would have lost anyway, and this way I will at least be consulted—"

"Talk to you a minute, Bob?" Buttermaker interrupted.

Whitewood disengaged from his audience and turned to Buttermaker. "How things going, Mo? Working the boys hard?"

"Bob, what's this garbage about uniforms?"

"What do you mean? Haven't you gotten them yet?"

"You never told me about them."

"You know the teams have to get sponsors for uniforms, certainly you know that, pal."

"Look, you're paying me to—"

"Ssssh!" Whitewood glanced around nervously. "I'm standing right next to you, for Chrissake. You don't have to announce it."

"You told me I'd be coaching these kids a couple of hours a day. I got pools to clean, for crying out loud, to make a living. I can't be running around looking for—"

"You've been hired as a manager," Whitewood whispered brusquely, "and that includes everything."

Buttermaker sighed and took a drink from his mug.

"And that includes," Whitewood went on, "getting a sponsor for uniforms."

"Who, for example?" Buttermaker asked sleepily.

"There are dozens of merchants in this town who would be only too happy to sponsor a . . ."

Buttermaker drifted away. The crowd in the main room had thinned, and jammed instead into a small side room where slides were being projected onto a wall. Buttermaker joined them, standing at the rear. The present slide was of the happy face of a boy in a red baseball cap. Roy Turner was narrating.

". . . that young Tommy was hit in the head by a pitched ball six years ago. He has had a tough time. As we all know"—Turner's voice choked for an instant—"he was one of the nicest boys ever to play in our league. A bunch of us thought it would be a nice idea if we named the new scoreboard after Tommy, just put his name up there with his team. Any objections?"

Several parents said, "No . . . good idea."

Buttermaker turned away and started back to the table for a refill.

"Any objections?" Jill Turner was at his elbow.

"No." He looked down at her. "Why should there be? Who was Tommy?"

"A Yankee," she said, "naturally."

Buttermaker, with long, graceful strides, nicked the inside of the bag at second and raced toward third, his Tiparillo clamped between his teeth. He dropped into a slide, lightly furrowing the dirt, and smoothly hooked the inside of the bag with his right foot.

"Wow!" said several wide-eyed Bears who were gathered around the base for the demonstration. "Like the PROS, man," said Ahmad.

"Fast," said Toby Whitewood.

"And perfect," added Lefty Stein.

"Looka those tire marks," said Engelberg, shaking his head. "I sure wish I could slide that far."

"But why do we have to quit practice early today, Coach?" Tanner asked. "That's what *I* wanna know."

"We have a pool to clean, my boy," Buttermaker said, dusting himself off.

"Whose?" Tanner was insistent.

Buttermaker narrowed his eyes to study him. "The Lazars'. What's it to you?"

"Just wondered," Tanner said. "I don't know nobody with a pool."

Buttermaker clapped his hands. "All right, boys, let's try it. Jose?" He waved his arm to indicate a slide.

Jose got down like a sprinter near second base and took off. His little legs churned up dirt as he barreled toward third, his mouth set in concentration. He threw up his arms and sank into a nice slide. When the dust cleared, he looked up at Buttermaker expectantly.

Buttermaker was standing ten feet away, on top of third base. "Good slide, Jose, but the idea is to get to the bag. "Okay, Lefty?"

Lefty Stein headed down the baseline with his head tilted back, long arms and legs flailing. When he neared third, he didn't slide so much as collapse, rolling, thrashing, spewing dirt in all directions. Buttermaker jumped to avoid him as he tumbled toward, over, and beyond the bag, ending up in a heap in the coach's box.

Buttermaker walked over and hoisted him up under the arms. "All right, we'll work on it." He clapped his hands. "Okay, that's it for today. Those who can join me at the pool, let's get the gear together and load up. Can't be late!"

The boys jammed into Buttermaker's Cadillac, sprawled on and around the pool-cleaning equipment.

THE BAD NEWS BEARS

The car bounced along unevenly on old shocks. A can of beer nestled between Buttermaker's legs.

Toby Whitewood leaned over the front seat, resting on his arms. "Coach, how could you possibly strike out Johnny Bench?"

"With a slider, my boy," Buttermaker said, "had a gem of a slider in those days."

"Toby means," said Ogilvie, who was seated beside Buttermaker, with a finger upraised, "that since Johnny Bench is a major leaguer, and we've established quite certainly that you never got beyond the Pacific Coast League, how could—"

"It was spring training, dammit," Buttermaker snapped. He reached across to the glove compartment and extracted the Jim Beam, deftly added it to the beer as he drove, and swigged. "Vero Beach, Florida. Struck him out a couple of times, slider low and away."

Tanner grunted. "Sounds like so much bull."

"Hmmph," Buttermaker said.

"Hey, you're not supposed to have open liquor in your car," Engelberg whined, bolting upright in the back and leaning forward. "It's against the law."

"So," said Buttermaker, "is punching a bear in his fat chops."

"If you were so great," Tanner said, "how come you never made it to the majors?"

Buttermaker hoisted his right arm. "The old elbow, Tanner. Bane of every pitcher, tennis player, shot-putter, and mailman. Calcium deposits, bursitis, arthritis, rheumatism, and pain cut short my career. Too many curves and sliders, threw too hard, wasted myself too early. Should have developed a knuckler, I wouldn't be cleaning pools today."

Tanner hissed softly as the car pulled into a tree-lined driveway. The appearance of a mansion suddenly captivated the boys' attention. They stared open-mouthed. Tanner scoffed. "People are people, nobody's different. Rich, poor, all the same—they all go down with a good punch."

Buttermaker drove through the property along a winding drive, pulled up next to a splendid, kidney-shaped pool, and parked.

The boys hauled out the equipment and lugged it over to poolside. "Snap to it, boys," Buttermaker said. "The quicker we're finished, the quicker we get to the range."

Buttermaker directed them to their tasks. Jimmy Feldman set to work vacuuming the bottom. Miguel and Jose mixed chlorine and acid. Ogilvie and Engelberg struggled to fit the filter in place. Other boys scrubbed down the sides.

The boys underway, Buttermaker toted a cooler out of the car trunk and set it down beside a lounge chair, into which he then settled himself. Timmy Lupus opened the cooler and began sorting out the contents.

"Ogilvie," Buttermaker called, lying back with eyes closed, "how's that filter coming?"

"Almost fixed."

"You're going to have a bright future in pools some day, Ogilvie."

"Hey, Tower!" Tanner's voice boomed from the depths of the pool, "Brush the SIDES, not ME!"

"So SORRY!"

"Hey, Coach?" came Lefty Stein's voice. "How could you possibly teach a nine-year-old girl how to throw a curve ball?"

"With patience and skill, my friend," Buttermaker answered cheerily, "and not only a curve, but the most vicious spitter you've ever seen."

"Hog slop," Tanner said.

Timmy Lupus, who had been pouring, measuring, and shaking the contents of the cooler, cautiously handed a paper cup to Buttermaker. He held his breath as Buttermaker took a sip.

"Superb, Lupus," said Buttermaker at last, smacking his lips, "superb. As dry, chilled, and quick as a martini should be."

Timmy smiled and blushed.

Buttermaker closed his eyes. "Yes, that's what you need to teach people, patience and skill. I took a little girl fresh out of hopscotch and gave her a curve ball that bent like a pretzel. I could even teach you boys something, if you just had, if I just had . . ."

Whereupon he dozed off.

Morris Buttermaker dreamed a bittersweet dream.

He sat on the porch of a small frame cottage, his arm around a beautiful, slender woman with long blond hair. They dangled their feet off the edge and watched a little girl climbing in the wispy branches of an evergreen tree in front.

"Your sister's quite the tomboy, Brenda," he said, hugging her tight.

Brenda lay her head on Buttermaker's shoulder. "She sure is. She's funny. She's really serious about having you teach her to pitch, you know."

"I figured. Well, why not?"

He went to his car and pulled out a baseball and two gloves. "Amanda," he called, "wanna pitch?"

Amanda jumped down from her branch and came running over. "You bet, Mo."

She resembled Brenda, though with shorter blond hair, which hung straight to her shoulders and drifted over her left eye. She was slender, and had Brenda's fine, high cheekbones and delicately formed nose. Her lips were lush and red, her smile enchanting. And her eyes were piercing blue and wide with innocence—she was indeed a miniature Brenda.

Except for her clothes. Brenda was always neat, proper; she tended to skirts and sweaters. Amanda wore a green T-shirt with ROLLING STONES stenciled on it, and dungarees with a hole in one knee. Her sneakers, which she wore without socks, were tattered. A long, superficial scratch, from some recent brush against a limb, ran up her left forearm. She was in constant motion, never still, bouncing up and down with overflow energy as she stood in front of Buttermaker.

He handed her a glove, which came up nearly to her elbow. He extended his hand with the ball. "Now, here's how you hold it for a curve, your fingers on the laces like this. I like to throw overhand, like so." He swung his arm over his head. "Now, the key is in snapping your elbow and wrist so you come down hard over the top of the ball when you release." He snapped his arm down, giving a sharp outward twist of his wrist. "That's basically it. The harder you snap it off, the sharper the curve. There's all speeds, all kinds of breaks. But you have to snap your elbow and wrist for every one. That's why they don't start out kids throwing curves, because it tears heck out of their arms if they start too early, before their muscles and bones are developed."

"So I guess you're telling me it's too early?" Amanda said, cocking her head and frowning.

"Naw, not you. Not unless you intend to pitch for the Tigers some day." Buttermaker chuckled.

"Well, I MIGHT."

"Sure, like *I* might."

"Well, you ALMOST did."

"Almost. Come on, go over by the fence and I'll

throw you a couple easy ones to show you how it works."

"You're not going to PITCH to her, Mo," Brenda said, nervously coming down the steps.

"Don't worry, just a couple slow, easy sinkers. Ready, Amanda?"

"Chuck it right to me, babe."

Buttermaker wound up with a lazy, smooth motion, and threw. The ball arched toward Amanda's glove, then abruptly dipped and hit the ground under it.

"Wow! Hey, sis, you see that?"

"Yes. Hey, Mo, it really DID curve."

"Heck yes, Brenda. Did you think curve balls were a myth?"

"I just never saw one close up."

"Okay, Amanda," Buttermaker said, "you know how they look. Here's strike two." He threw, and again the ball ducked and bounced at Amanda's feet.

"Wow! I can't wait to do that."

"Wanna try some?"

"Sure."

Buttermaker crouched down and held up his glove as a target. Amanda planted her right foot forward and went into a windup—not as gawky as Buttermaker had expected, but too hurried—and, with an arm motion that was half throw and half push, let loose a soft but straight pitch.

"Okay, slow down, relax the windup. And snap your wrist, lead your arm with that."

Amanda threw again, this time with a more fluid motion of her arm, but still with no curve.

"Better. Good motion. Snap the wrist now."

Amanda threw again and again, her arm swinging ever more easily and smoothly. Still no curve.

Buttermaker was surprised at how naturally she took

to throwing. Maybe one day she actually WOULD throw a curve. He chuckled at that unlikely possibility. "Rest a while," he said, tossing her the ball.

Amanda didn't rest. She continued to throw by herself against the fence.

Buttermaker and Brenda went inside and sat together on the sofa, leaning against each other. They sipped Scotch-and-sodas.

"You've very comfortable here, aren't you, Mo?" she asked.

"Like a weevil in cotton."

"You could stay, you know."

"I DO, sometimes, in case you've forgotten."

She smiled and punched him playfully in the shoulder. "Oh, silly, I mean STAY, you know. Amanda loves you."

"As if SHE were the point."

Brenda giggled. "I just mean, you know, I COULD have a little sister that didn't like you, or you didn't like, that would complicate things. But the three of us are so comfortable together."

"That we are, my dear."

"And you and I, we love each other too."

"I don't trust love."

"You're such a liar, Mo," she said, tweaking his nose.

"Two sisters shouldn't live together," he said. "I mean, when you're grown up. I mean, you should have a place alone."

"And Amanda?"

"She should get married."

She giggled again. "It's ME that should get married, Mo."

"Mmm."

"And you, you should get married."

43

"Wow, imagine me married."

Brenda got up and stood in front of him. "I want to marry you, Mo," she said quietly.

"Why not? I'm a heck of a catch."

"Blast it, Mo," Brenda said angrily, clenching her fists. "Why do you have to joke all the time? What's the matter with you? It's no joke for people like us to get married."

"I'm sorry, I didn't mean to joke. It's just that, well . . ."

"Just that what, Mo?"

"Just that I can't see myself married. I don't think I could handle the, the responsibility, or the—"

"There's nobody else you would rather be with?"

"No, of course not."

"No place else you'd rather be?"

"No."

Brenda started to cry. "The trouble with you, Mo, is you don't want anybody. You don't even want to be wanted. You want to be a lonely nobody." She turned away and leaned her head against the wall, shaking with sobs. "I'm fed up, Mo."

He finished his drink and looked at her. He clasped his hands together and looked at them. He shut his eyes and took a deep breath. "What do you mean by that?"

"I mean," she said without facing him, "that I'm fed up with this part-time stuff, finished, unless you will face the fact that we could be happy being married. You won't admit that, even to yourself. So you might just as well leave and be lonely by yourself."

He studied his empty glass. "You don't mean that," he said softly.

"I do."

He turned the glass slowly in his hands. "Okay." He

stood up. For a long moment he stared at the back of her head through moist eyes. The happiest days of his life had been with her. "Okay." He picked up his pitcher's glove and walked out, slowly closing the door behind him. He walked down the steps to the yard.

"Hey, Mo!" Amanda yelled to him. "I got it! I really got it! Here, catch this!"

Buttermaker wiped his eyes. "Okay." He crouched down and gave Amanda a target with his glove. Amanda went into an exaggerated windup and delivered. The ball looped slowly toward him, then broke downward. He caught it at his shoe tops, and stood up smiling.

Amanda was jumping up and down and pounding her fist into her glove gleefully.

Buttermaker shook his head and laughed. He tossed her the ball. "Here, keep it, work on it. You're right, pitch, you got it. It'll be breaking two feet in a week. See you later."

Amanda caught the ball and went running toward the cottage. "Sis! Sis! I got it! I can throw a curve! Sis . . ."

Buttermaker was rudely awakened by a scream from the pit of the swimming pool.

"Shut up, Engelberg, or I'll punch you again!" The voice following the scream was Tanner's.

Buttermaker hoisted himself up painfully and stumbled to the edge of the pool. Engelberg's face was a mass of oozing red. "What the hell!" Buttermaker yelled, starting down the steps backward.

Voices came at him from all directions.

"All Engelberg said was—"

"That all the Yankees have pools—"

"And so maybe we'd all be better off—"

"Making friends with the Yankees, so we could use their pools—"

"Instead of—"

"INSTEAD OF BEATING THEM!" Tanner hollered. "That's what the blimp said."

Buttermaker lurched across the pool bottom toward Engelberg. "Well, for Pete's sake, Tanner," he said, "you don't punch a guy in the mouth for THAT."

"He didn't punch him in the mouth, Coach," said Ogilvie. "Actually, he punched him in the SANDWICH, which happened to be cranberry and ketchup."

Buttermaker arrived at the sobbing Engelberg and saw that the red gore which covered his face was in fact cranberry and ketchup, and not blood. He wiped off Engelberg's face with his handkerchief, and made a gift of the handkerchief to Engelberg. "Here, wash it," Buttermaker said. "Okay, if we're finished, let's get out to the range."

The Bears loaded the gear into the Cadillac, clambered in after it, and were off.

They pulled into a parking area under a large sign that read, ENCINO BATTING RANGE: 10 SWINGS FOR A QUARTER.

The Bears spilled out and scampered to the batting cage. Buttermaker went over to the booth and handed a ten-dollar bill to a silent, beefy man munching a taco. Then he went back to the car, opened a can of beer, laced it with Jim Beam, and carried it with him to the batting cage.

Ahmad was already in, ready to hit. The automatic pitching machine sent one his way. Ahmad bared his teeth, shut his eyes, and lunged at the ball, missing it by several feet.

"Even Hank Aaron peels open the old eyelids before

he takes a cut, Ahmad," Buttermaker said, seating himself on the ground and taking a swig.

"What about our uniforms, Mr. Buttermaker?" asked Toby Whitewood.

"I'm working on it, kid," Buttermaker said, testily.

"Maybe I should swish-hit, try it left-handed," Ahmad called out.

Buttermaker took another swig. "Not just yet, Ahmad."

"All the other teams have their uniforms already," whined Lefty Stein. "When are you—"

"You guys worry about baseball," Buttermaker growled, "and let me worry about uniforms." He took another long drink, then lay down on the ground and fell asleep.

The comic parade of batting Bears continued. Lefty swung and missed, lost his balance, and crashed into the wire cage. Timmy Lupus, confused by the pitching machine, stood still as a statue, with the bat on his shoulder, as several pitches sailed by.

"You dumb crud," Tanner said, "give somebody else a turn if you're just gonna stand there!"

Ogilvie tried to direct the machine as he readied the bat to swing. "Wait a minute, wait a minute," he kept saying as the pitches kept coming.

Engelberg nicked off two fouls with mighty swings, then lost his bat on the third, sending it crashing into the pitching machine.

At that, the man in the booth came running out and, seeing Buttermaker asleep flat on his back, called a halt to the practice.

Buttermaker sat up and rubbed his eyes. Timmy Lupus, sitting next to him, handed him an opened can of beer. Buttermaker took it. "Thanks, kid," he said, "I needed that."

Buttermaker tried all over town, without success, to get a sponsor for uniforms. The man at Ye Olde Modern Hardware said he wasn't interested in games. The man at Valley Sporting Gds. and Picnic Equip. was sponsoring another team. The man at Julio's Barber Shop said he didn't understand English. The man at Safety Drip-Dry Laundry said it was all he could do to make a living. And so it went.

Whatever frustration Buttermaker felt at being unable to secure a sponsor was doubled at the Bears' practice sessions. Sometimes he laughed, sometimes he raged, sometimes he just watched helplessly. Balls hit to the outfield took several minutes to find and return; balls hit to the infield bounced into heads, noses, bellies, instead of gloves; balls thrown from one base to another ended up by or beyond the fence. As for batting practice, nobody could touch the ball, unless hit by it, which they often were, so wild was the pitching. A foul ball was a good day. The Bears were battered, bruised, and nearly beaten before they started.

They were growing more depressed daily, and as a result more sluggish. Buttermaker decided that, since playing ball didn't seem to help, he would at least get them into shape.

He paced back and forth before his team, which he had lined up in front of the dugout. He eyed them sternly, and swished his beer can back and forth. "All right. Bears, as Willie Mays once said to me—"

"I suppose you struck him out too," Engelberg mumbled.

"Button up, Engelberg," Buttermaker said, giving him a cold eye. "As Willie said to me, 'No ballplayer can perform to capacity unless—' "

"Geez!"

"—unless he is in TOP PHYSICAL CONDITION!'
That's right. And that includes us Bears. And so—"

"How about the coach?"

Buttermaker looked quickly around the group, unable to locate the source of the comment. "And so, we
will now run LAPS! Ten laps around the fence. Let's
go, NOW!"

Buttermaker took off at a brisk trot, followed by his
groaning, whining team.

After three laps, Buttermaker stood aside, gasping, to
watch from the pitcher's mound. Ogilvie and Engelberg
were lagging far behind, and he saw them sneak toward
a hole in the fence.

"Back in the race, you two!" he hollered. "Or else
the whole team takes more laps!"

Faced with the ominous prospect of such peer pres-
sure, the two laggards got back into the strung-out line of
panting Bears.

Alone in the parking lot, seated on his Harley, was
the boy Buttermaker had seen on his first day. For a
while the boy just sat, watching the Bears run laps.
Then his gaze met Buttermaker's, and, over that distance, their eyes locked briefly as if in some strange
challenge. Then the boy cranked up and sped away.

One by one, the Bears finished their laps and fell to
the ground, panting and moaning. Buttermaker strode
among the prostrate bodies. "Boys, be here a little early
tomorrow. I may have a surprise for you."

"Pushups!" gasped Engelberg.

"Maybe," Buttermaker said. "Not a bad idea."

As the Bears headed toward the bicycle rack, Buttermaker sidled up to Tanner. "Say, Tanner, who was that
boy on the motorcycle?"

"He's Kelly Leak, Coach—nobody you'd want to
know."

It was just two days before the opening game of the season. Buttermaker stumbled blindly toward the dugout behind the stack of cardboard boxes he was carrying.

"You're twenty minutes late," Tanner said, miffed, "after you told us to be here early."

"Right," said Buttermaker. He dumped the boxes onto the ground in front of the waiting players.

"What's that?"

"What's in the boxes?"

"What you've been waiting for," Buttermaker said happily. "Open 'em up."

The boys lunged for the boxes and ripped them open, and pulled out their uniforms, gray with purple trim, and purple caps.

"Oooh!"

"Wow!"

"Man!"

"What the heck's THAT?" Tanner asked, holding up a shirt and pointing to the lettering on the back.

Stenciled there was

CHICO'S BAIL BONDS

"What's bail bonds?" Toby Whitewood asked.

"To save up money and support the government, stupid," Lefty said.

"I'm afraid you're in error there," said Ogilvie, pointing his index finger skyward. "What you're thinking of is U.S. Savings Bonds. Actually, these bonds are for people who are arrested and—"

"What these are," said Buttermaker, snatching the shirt from Tanner, "are uniforms, you snot-noses. And if you don't like them, I can just take them back and—"

"Who gives a hang about the words," said Tanner, grabbing the shirt back. "They're OUR uniforms, and they're beautiful!"

"Right!"

"Right on!"

"They're beautiful!"

Last practice before their first game. Buttermaker sat weaving back and forth on the pitcher's mound, lobbing balls in for batting practice. Between each pitch he took a drink from one of the beer cans that filled the paper bag beside him.

Engelberg tried to bunt, and the ball hit him in his soft belly.

Ahmad swung so hard in missing that he spun around twice, fell down, got up, and staggered dizzily into Timmy Lupus.

Ogilvie was inhaling asthma spray when a soft pitch knocked the tube from under his nose and sent it skittering to the backstop.

Jose swung viciously and popped one straight up. He stood looking around for the ball until it dropped on his head.

Buttermaker's pitches, from his seated position, grew more and more unpredictable, and batters hopped all around the home-plate area trying to reach them. Buttermaker chuckled as he threw and watched the boys dance after the ball.

"Come on, Coach," Tanner said grumpily, "this ain't no joke."

Buttermaker tossed one high into the air and watched it drop toward the backstop as Regi Tower chased it, swinging the bat wildly back and forth in a vain attempt to hit it, until both the ball and Regi fell in the dirt.

"May I refer you, Tanner," Buttermaker said, giggling, "to a fine book by Saroyan called *The Human Comedy*, in which is demonstrated the fact"—he lobbed another pitch high into the sky—"that all life's jokes have their base in tragedy, that what is laughable to some is most sad to . . . to . . ." Buttermaker slung a pitch that bounced into the dugout; then he toppled over and passed out.

The Bears gathered around his still form, shaking their heads and muttering curses.

"What do we do now?" asked Jimmy Feldman.

"Nothing," said Engelberg. "He ain't no good to us when he's sober either."

"Who knows?" Ahmad said. "We ain't never seen him that way."

Tanner stomped back and forth in a rage, spitting to either side. "Opening day is TOMORROW! We ain't even got our positions set, or the batting order, or ANYTHING!" He stalked over to Buttermaker's inert body and gave it a prod with his foot. "All we got's a drunken, lousy, crud, boozer, CRAZY COACH!" He kicked the paper bag, sending cans and spume over the pitcher's mound.

"What do we do?"

"We can't just leave him here."

"Somebody get some coffee."

"Let's carry him off the field at least, so we can practice."

Several Bears grabbed Buttermaker's arms and legs and tried to hoist him up. Suddenly a shadow loomed over them. They looked up at the scowling face of Roy Turner.

"Uh . . ."

"We was just . . ."

"He's just taking a nap . . ."

"We didn't want to wake him . . ."

"BEAT IT!" Turner shouted.

At that instant, Jose and Miguel raced up from the snack bar, carrying four styrofoam cups of spilling, steaming coffee. They froze, hiding the coffee behind them.

Turner scooped up Buttermaker, tossed him over his shoulder, and carried him into the snack bar.

Buttermaker sat unsteadily on the edge of the counter, his legs dangling lifelessly below, his chin resting on his chest. In his hands he slowly turned a cup of coffee, from which he occasionally sipped.

"Feeling better?" Roy Turner asked, leaning against the opposite wall with his arms folded.

"Yeah."

Turner walked over. "Good." Then he swung a stiff right hand into Buttermaker's chest, knocking him off the counter and onto the floor, where he lay groaning.

"You irresponsible drunk!" Turner spat at him. "Ever occur to you what kind of EXAMPLE you are to these boys? While I spend my time driving my team, pushing 'em to the limit, making winners out of them, you spend your time being a LUSH!"

Buttermaker scrambled painfully to all fours. "You shouldn't punch people, Turner, especially people in this condition."

"Get outta my sight, you phony HAS-BEEN!"

Buttermaker struggled to his feet and stumbled out of the snack bar. For a few moments he leaned against the outside wall. When his eyes focused, he saw that the Bears were still there, sitting in the dugout, waiting for him. "Pint-sized jerks," he muttered to himself. He dragged himself out to the field.

The Bears emerged hesitantly from the dugout and surrounded him.

"Timmy," he said, coughing, "go to the car, bring me a beer."

Timmy started to trot toward the parking lot, but Jimmy Feldman grabbed his arm. "No, Timmy," he said, looking at Buttermaker. "You've had enough, Coach."

"Don't mess with me," Buttermaker said, coughing again. "I'm not in the mood."

Ogilvie stepped up to Buttermaker's side and adjusted his glasses. "Jimmy's point is well taken, Coach Buttermaker. Today your consumption has exceeded what would be called the—"

"Dammit, Ogilvie!" Buttermaker said. "Will you shut up and quit trying to talk like a college professor!" He nodded his head at Timmy and fluttered his hand toward the parking lot. "Go ahead, Lupus."

Timmy looked from face to face among the Bears, as each in turn shook his head, no. He screwed up his face as if in pain, and danced nervously on one foot, then the other.

"I said get going, before I—" Buttermaker doubled up, coughing. Timmy took the chance to duck behind several players.

Tanner stepped forward. "We're sick of this, Buttermaker. We been bragging to everybody how great you are, how you struck out Johnny Bench, how you showed a nine-year-old girl how to throw curves, and—"

Ahmad stepped up shoulder to shoulder with Tanner. "And how you were gonna mold us into a WINNING TEAM!"

"Yeah," said Tanner. "But now we're fed up. When you gonna start coaching?"

"Never!" shouted Buttermaker, looking away from them. The boys stared at him, stunned. "Because you're UNCOACHABLE!" He lowered his voice a bit. "Stop kidding yourselves. Leo Durocher himself couldn't do anything with this team. Ballplayers are born, not taught."

Now Buttermaker turned to look at the boys. Many had tears in their eyes. He hadn't expected that. But neither had they expected such words from him.

Ahmad looked at the ground and fidgeted with his glove. "Well," he said softly, "we all born the way we born. 'Cludin you, Coach. Can't none of us do nothin' about that. We just willin' to try to play ball, that's all."

There was a long silence, during which Buttermaker stirred uncomfortably and coughed often. He faced away from them. "Well, you can all go home now. Practice is over. I got a pool to clean today anyway. And tomorrow, we all got a game."

The Bears drifted off, all of them downcast, moving together toward the bicycle rack, leaving Buttermaker standing alone on the pitcher's mound, his back to them.

Morris Buttermaker sat down on the pitcher's mound facing home plate, his arms around his knees and his head down. He sat there for a long time as the shadows of the fence spread in across the outfield grass toward him. Gradually the fuzziness in his mind dissipated like an early-morning fog, and as it did it was replaced by a cloudy misery.

Physically, of course, he felt awful. It was common too that mental depression accompanied the physical discomfort from alcoholic hangover. But he felt worse than usual.

He knew that he was neither a mean man nor a cruel one, and yet here with these boys he had displayed unmistakable meanness and cruelty. He knew it was out of frustration, but that was no excuse. Cruelty was most often people's expression of frustration.

He remembered a time in high school—a recollection so long hidden from himself that he couldn't recall even the team they had been playing—when he had a no-hitter going in the last inning. It would be his fourth no-hitter of the season, a league record. The batter hit a high pop-foul just behind home plate. The catcher dropped it. Given new life, the batter hit the next pitch to left for a single.

The catcher walked slowly out to the mound and handed Buttermaker the ball.

Buttermaker now recalled how cruelly he had glared at his battery mate. He had said to him: "I hope you remember that play the rest of your life."

"I'm sorry," the catcher had replied sadly, "I wanted that one as bad as you."

So now it was Buttermaker who remembered it. Fair enough. He had apologized profusely to the catcher after the game (which they had won anyway), and they had slapped each other on the back. The incident, he had thought, was forgotten.

But you don't atone for mistreatment of people by apologies. You atone by learning not to mistreat them again. Buttermaker felt that he never learned anything soon enough about people. As a pitcher, he had had so much talent that he was often impatient with teammates who had less. But he seldom expressed that impatience outwardly in his treatment of his teammates. What he did instead, through the years, was let his talent fade. He had quickly become a highly touted pro, and almost as quickly begun to let his arm go to waste. He preferred, though he didn't entirely recognize the fact, to be able to blame himself for losses. It was easier, more private, caused him less remorse, than to blame others.

But here he felt so helpless. He wasn't pitching, he was coaching. He didn't know how to bring this woebegone team to life, and so, in frustration, he had said mean things to them. At least he could blame himself for that.

The light had become so dim that he could barely make out the backstop. He felt more comfortable in the darkness, more alone. Perhaps the boys would forget what he had said. If they won their game tomorrow, perhaps they would forget. For that, they needed a miracle. They deserved one.

CHAPTER 3

A half-hour before game time on opening day, the parking lot was jammed, as were the two small sets of bleachers behind each of the opposing dugouts. Among the parents in the stands were sprinkled players of various teams scheduled for later games and games the next day. They wore their uniforms of red, green, blue, orange, adding a festive coloration to the bustling spectator crowd which sat in shirt-sleeves under the bright sun. Several fathers accompanied their proud sons strutting in from the parking lot, continuing to swell the crowd.

A band of twenty pieces wearing blue marching outfits with white-plumed hats stood in four ranks beside the flagpole in center field, playing "Yankee Doodle Dandy."

An announcer's voice droned in the background, repeating names of opposing players and coaches, ground rules, the snack-bar menu, and general information about the league and the game.

Kelly Leak chugged into the parking lot, swerving unsteadily on his Harley. His eyes had a glaze, and he

drank from a canteen. He pulled alongside three de-
mure girls and spoke to them. The girls stepped up their
pace, their noses high in the air.

Buttermaker leaned against the drinking fountain, occasionally popping an aspirin into his mouth and following it with a long drink of water. His eyes were
heavily lidded, puffy, and red. He coughed often, and
blew his nose.

Over near the snack bar, Councilman Whitewood
was holding court with a small group of parents, pointing out various things around the field to them, nodding, patting people on the back, shaking hands with
passers-by.

A few minutes before game time, a photographer,
with a bulky old Speed Graphic dangling from his hand,
approached Buttermaker.

"Somebody said you haven't got your team picture
yet," he said. "I guess we better do it now."

Buttermaker nodded, walked over to the dugout, and
waved the Bears together. They followed him out to
center field near the flagpole. The photographer arranged them in two rows, the front one kneeling. He
handed those in front a white paper banner on which
was printed BEARS in purple crayon.

Having finally got them arranged and still, the photographer directed them to smile. Some did, some did
not. Buttermaker stood with arms folded, staring dully
into the camera as the flashbulb went off.

"Good enough," said the photographer after one
shot.

All of a sudden, there was a roar from the parking
lot. Kelly Leak churned onto the outfield grass aboard
his Harley. Grass and dirt sprayed from his rear wheel
as he slid onto the base paths. Leaning hard over and
dragging his inside foot, Kelly skidded around the entire

diamond, bouncing over each base. Then he headed straight for the center-field fence. The Bears scattered. Just short of the fence, Kelly attempted to spin around in a circle, but he lost control of the bike and slid instead into the base of the fence, slamming loose several boards, and he tumbled off and lay dazed.

A policeman, who had been pursuing him on foot in a losing race around the bases, now ran up to him, lifted him to his feet, and steadied him. Then, with one hand in a firm grip on Kelly's shoulder and the other hand guiding the smoking Harley, he walked the dirt-smeared boy over to the patrol car in the parking lot.

The event had stilled the crowd for a few minutes. But, with the apprehension and removal of the perpetrator, their enthusiasm quickly returned.

The two opposing teams in the first game lined up along the base paths for the National Anthem, the Yankees along third, the Bears along first. The well-drilled Yankees stood stiffly in a neat row, uniformly holding their red-trimmed caps over their hearts. The Bears formed a scraggly, snaky, twitching line, and only with a good deal of elbowing and shoving did they succeed in getting one another to take their caps off.

A local soprano sang a reasonable "Star-Spangled Banner" a beat behind the band. Then the umpire and several parents shouted, "PLAY BALL!"

The Bears took the field. The Agilar boys, at first and second bases, waved happily to their wildly applauding parents in the stands. Tanner Boyle kicked dirt and spat in his glove at shortstop. Regi Tower stood motionless at third base. Jimmy Feldman in left, Toby Whitewood in center, and Ahmad Rahim in right all pounded fists into their gloves. Lefty Stein threw the last of his warm-up pitches, several of which a sweating

Mike Engelberg was forced to retrieve from the back-stop.

Roy Turner stood near the plate with his arm around his first Yankee batter, whispering instructions.

Buttermaker leaned back in the dugout, his legs crossed to conceal a can of beer. On either side of him, hunched forward intently, were Timmy Lupus and Ogil-vie.

The batter stepped into the box. Lefty labored into a gawky windup and delivered the first pitch of the season. The batter took the first swing and smacked a ground ball toward Miguel, at second. It bounced off his shoulder and rolled into center field.

The Yankees were out of their dugout, cheering, as the batter rounded first and headed for second. Toby charged the ball and heaved it on a bounce to Tanner, covering the bag. Tanner, his eye distracted by the ap-proaching runner, missed it entirely, and the ball rolled to the pitcher's mound.

"THIRD!" Roy Turner yelled to the runner. "GO TO THIRD!"

Lefty, finally awakening to the situation, grabbed the ball hard with his gloved hand. Too hard—the ball stuck in the webbing. He tried to shake it out. He took off his glove and flailed it savagely to dislodge the ball. It dropped to the ground and rolled just behind his feet. He spun crazily, trying to find it.

"HOME! GO HOME!"

At last Lefty spotted the ball and threw a strike to Engelberg, who squatted over home plate like a Bud-dha. Engelberg caught the ball just as the runner piled into him and knocked him over backward. The ball tumbled from his mitt and rolled to the backstop.

"SAFE!" bellowed the umpire, leaning in close over the tangled opponents.

The Yankees were doubled up with laughter, slapping one another's backs. Some laughter came from the stands, too.

In the dugout, Ogilvie picked up the score sheet and scratched in a *1* for the Yankees. Buttermaker walked back and forth, clapping his hands and yelling encouragement at the embarrassed Bears, who were staring at the ground. "Come on! We'll get it back! One little run! Look alive! No batter up there, no batter!"

The Bears responded with a few shrugs and grunts, and returned to their positions. "Come on, Stein," muttered Tanner.

Joey Turner, the Bears' nemesis during practice sessions, stepped up to the plate. Lefty gritted his teeth and clamped his lips together. He glared at the batter he was most determined to get. He wound up and fired. Turner drove it on a line over the left-field fence for a home run.

The jubilant Yankees were beside themselves, leaping and screeching, dancing and hugging. Roy Turner raised a fist in the air and pounded it on his son's shoulder as Joey proudly trotted around third.

Lefty waited with his head down as the ball was tossed back in over the fence, relayed and dropped, relayed and dropped, and finally handed to him by Regi Tower.

"Hang in there, Bears," called Buttermaker from the dugout, with less conviction than before.

But there followed a series of disasters which drained even the Yankees of laughter.

A pop fly was raised between first and second.

"*La Mia,*" Miguel called.

"*La Mia,*" Jose called.

They slammed together and bounced apart as the ball

landed between them and the runner landed on second base.

More hits, more runs.

A fly ball soared to right. Ahmad charged fiercely, then watched with dismay as the ball hit twenty feet behind him.

Several soda cans and half a hot dog sailed out onto the field from the stands. Several parents scolded their sons, and the umpire waved a menacing finger toward them. Buttermaker and Ogilvie and Timmy picked up the debris and dropped it into a trash can near the dugout.

Several more Yankees came to the plate, and smacked either clean hits or balls that slid, looped, and hopped among various Bears diving, stumbling, falling, tripping in valiant attempts to at least slow them down.

Still top of the first, no outs.

At the new scoreboard above the center-field fence, a boy, perched atop a ladder placed just outside, reached around to hang up the number *9,* then, moments later, *10.* As he reached to hang up *11,* a home-run ball smashed into the scoreboard just over his nose, sending the scorekeeper diving behind the fence for protection.

In the stands, the atmosphere was like a circus, with players from other teams tossing things at one another, laughing, braying, ducking, crawling around.

In contrast, several of the Bears tried to hide tears, wiping them quickly off their cheeks with their gloves.

A hard-hit ball bounced up the middle just to the right of the mound. Tanner dove for it vainly. He got up, sputtering and fuming, to take the throw in from Toby in center. Tanner's elbow dripped blood. Buttermaker ran out from the dugout. Tanner waved him away angrily.

Roy Turner, standing in the coach's box at third, shook his head and looked at his watch.

A high-bouncer headed toward Regi Tower, at third. Regi backed up, and backed up, and backed up, then fell over backward as the ball hopped over his head.

"I told you to CHARGE the darn thing!" came a shout from the stands.

A fly ball went deep to right. This time Ahmad followed the flight of the ball and drifted back, all the way to the fence. He stuck up his glove. The ball hit it and bounced off, over the fence for another homer.

Ahmad turned his face against the fence and stood quietly.

Top of the first, no outs, 20–0 Yankees. By now the stands were quiet, and the Bears made no attempt to hide their tears.

Buttermaker observed all this from his seat in the dugout, his chin in his hands. Ogilvie and Timmy glanced at him occasionally, looking for any sign of help.

Another ground ball down the third-base line was turned into a homer.

Buttermaker roused himself with a sigh and strolled out to the pitcher's mound. He gathered the infielders around him and took the ball from Lefty, tossing it up and down in his hand.

"Boys, maybe we should, oh, well, I think we've had enough for today."

He turned and walked to home plate. He was joined there by the umpire and Roy Turner. "Let's call it off," Buttermaker said.

Turner glanced around at his team and smiled. He put his arm around Buttermaker's shoulders. "Look, Buttermaker, they'll call this thing off by the rules in about fifteen minutes anyway. Let's let them finish it in the proper way."

"I say now," Buttermaker said.

"I'm just thinking of your boys," Turner said in a kind voice.

Buttermaker eyed him coldly. "Just out of curiosity, Turner, what's the league record for runs scored in one inning?"

"Uh, something like twenty-two."

"And you've got twenty-one." Buttermaker handed the ball to the umpire. "Game's over." He turned to walk away.

Turner, his fists clenched at his sides, whispered loudly after him: "This makes me just as sick as you, Buttermaker! Some pig-headed city councilman gets it into his mind to be a do-goody for a bunch of no-talent kids, and look what happens!"

Buttermaker continued walking away, and waved the Bears off the field just as the announcer's voice came over the public-address system:

"Parents and friends. The remainder of this game has been canceled by the request of the Bears' coach, and is forfeited to the Yankees. Next up, the Athletics and the Mets. The snack bar is . . ."

The Bears started off the field in a walk, then went into a trot, then a run; then they broke in a mad dash in all directions to get out of sight. Ahmad climbed over the right-field fence and disappeared.

Some of the boys took refuge with Buttermaker in the dugout. He tried to smile at them. They were dirty, sweaty, teary, ragged. But they tried to smile back.

"It's not so bad," Buttermaker said. "I was on a high-school team once that . . ." He coughed and shook his head. "It's only a game," he said.

The boys looked soberly at Buttermaker through blurred eyes.

"Actually," Ogilvie said, "the Yankees didn't beat us so much as we beat ourselves, so . . ."

Joey Turner of the Yankees stuck his head around the end of the dugout. "Maybe next time," he said, giggling, "you'll get a chance to bat."

Tanner leaped up and took a wild swing, but Joey had ducked out of sight. Buttermaker pulled Tanner back by the seat of his pants.

The team filed out of the dugout. Jimmy Feldman came running up and tugged at Buttermaker's arm. "It's Ahmad," he said breathlessly, "you gotta come and talk to him. He climbed up a tree. He won't come down. I promised I wouldn't tell his brothers."

Buttermaker followed Jimmy at a trot around the edge of the fence and deep into the park behind it, to a large oak tree. Ahmad, dressed only in his underpants, sat on a branch about fifteen feet up, sobbing heavily.

Buttermaker stared up at him, then down at his uniform, which lay in a heap on the ground, and scratched his head. "How's the view up there, Ahmad?"

Ahmad shook his head.

"Well, why aren't you wearing your clothes?"

"Don't deserve to . . . wear . . . no uniform," Ahmad said between sobs and hiccups.

Buttermaker gathered up the uniform and began to climb the tree.

"You get away from here, Buttermaker!" Ahmad yelled, holding tightly to his branch.

"This ain't your tree, Ahmad," Buttermaker said, continuing up, "anyone can climb it."

He reached a branch a few feet below Ahmad and sat precariously on it. "You're keeping your family waiting, you know."

"Don't wanna see 'em. Can't, hic, face 'em."

"Why not?"

"Why not? Why NOT! Errors! EASY FLY BALLS!" He reached up as if to catch one, and almost lost his balance. "That's why not."

"Those weren't easy fly balls, Ahmad. The sun was right in your eyes. And anyway, your brothers will understand."

Ahmad resumed sobbing. "No they WON'T. They was both big athletes, captains, ALL-STARS. And I'm not. I'm lousy at football, lousy at basketball, and lousy at baseball. I ain't worth nothin' to no team at all. So I quit."

Buttermaker cleared his throat and rubbed his hand over his mouth. "Well," he said calmly, "thank God Hank Aaron didn't think like that."

"Like WHAT? He was a captain and a all-star. He wasn't no—"

"Forty-two errors."

"Hunh?"

"Come off it, Ahmad, you know all about Aaron. You must know that the first year he played he committed forty-two errors. Darn near broke his heart. But he said, 'I ain't ever gonna quit.' And lucky for us he didn't, because the Babe's record would still be standing, and there'd be no great old number forty-four . . ."

"Where you hear all that?"

Buttermaker shrugged. "It's common knowledge."

"Is it the truth?" Ahmad peered intently down at Buttermaker.

"Ask Ogilvie."

"I ain't askin' Ogilvie. I'm askin you, 'cause you the coach."

Buttermaker looked down for a moment, then up at

Ahmad, locking eyes with him. "Here's the absolute truth, Ahmad: Hank Aaron decided when he was a kid that he wasn't gonna be a quitter."

Ahmad stared down at him, blinking hard.

Buttermaker turned away and sighed. "Well, too bad, because that kind of ruins some of my plans. I thought that maybe by about the fourth or fifth game you might be switch-hitting, if you still wanted to, but—"

"You said we was UNCOACHABLE."

"I was under the influence, my boy, and people do strange—"

"What's that, under the influence?"

"Oh, it can mean a lot of different things, Ahmad, almost anything. But mainly it means that you say stupid things. In any case, I was figuring that with your speed, I could start using you for bunts, but I guess—"

"You think I'm fast?"

"Lightning."

Ahmad started to climb down. "Forty-two errors, hunh?" He hung from the bottom branch and dropped to the ground. "Lightning." He pulled on his pants. "I forgot about bunts."

They walked together back to the side of the stands, where Ahmad's two brothers stood waiting. They smiled when they saw Ahmad, who was buttoning his shirt. One of the brothers ran over and grabbed him and tossed him playfully over his shoulder.

"Sun was in my eyes, you know," Ahmad said.

"We were just saying the same," the second brother said, slapping Ahmad's leg. "Let's go get us a hot dog."

Buttermaker slid wearily into his car. He noticed a package on the seat, wrapped clumsily in brown paper and tied with a purple ribbon. He opened it and found two cans of beer, a pack of Tiparillos, and a note. The note, carefully handwritten, said: "To the best coach in the world from your friend Timmy Lupus. Good luck opening day."

Buttermaker took one of the beers and snapped up the pull-tab. He took the Jim Beam from the glove compartment, added some to the can, and sat drinking while the second game of the day, between the Athletics and the Mets, began.

Buttermaker followed Councilman Whitewood down the City Hall corridor at a brisk walk.

Whitewood waved at a pretty secretary and then at a uniformed policeman, without slackening his pace.

"I just never expected anything like that," Whitewood said over his shoulder to Buttermaker. "Jesus, what a beating! My poor kid wouldn't come out of his room all weekend."

They entered Whitewood's spacious, cluttered office. The phone rang, and Whitewood picked it up while seating himself in his swivel chair behind his broad desk. He muttered a few brief comments to the caller and hung up.

Buttermaker remained standing. "Have you told the boys yet?" he asked.

The phone rang again. Whitewood answered, said to hold his calls for five minutes, and hung up.

"What?" he said to Buttermaker.

"I said, have you told the boys yet?"

"Not yet." Whitewood reached into a drawer and pulled out a large checkbook. "I was hoping to sneak away from the office this afternoon and stop by the field." He wrote out a check. "But I'm gonna be tied up. I was thinking it might be better coming from you anyway, since you're their coach." He handed the check to Buttermaker.

Buttermaker took it and looked at it. "What if they don't want to quit?"

"They want to quit, all right," Whitewood said. "It's the best thing."

"For them? Or for you and me?"

Whitewood swiveled around to face out the window. A shaft of the midday sun beat in on him, and he squinted into it. "Well, for all of us, I guess. Sure, I wanted Toby to be able to play on a team. And he just couldn't make any of the six teams there were. But I wanted those other boys to have a team to play on too. Now it's obvious that we put them in over their heads. They just aren't cut out to play baseball."

"I was thinking the other day," Buttermaker said, scratching his head and gazing pensively at Whitewood's back, "about high school."

"Hmmm?"

"About when I told the coach at Central that you were a terrific center-fielder, when you actually had never played a game outside of sandlot before. And he put you in, let you start, our fourth game, I think it was. Remember?"

Whitewood spun to face him. "Of course I remember. And I did all right, didn't I?"

"You did all right because you didn't have to make a play for three games. You didn't have to make a play because I didn't allow a ball to be hit out of the infield. And remember how we used to sneak out after practices, just you and me, so I could hit fly balls out to you, make you run all over the place, until you finally got the hang of it?"

Whitewood stared at him.

"Remember, Bob? And before anybody knew how bad you were, you were good, darn good. Then a star at

71

college and all that. Long time ago, hunh? Easy to forget."

"I haven't forgotten any of that, Mo. But I had some natural talent, you've got to admit."

"At the time, I frankly didn't know if you had talent or not. But you were my friend. And I knew that if my luck held out, I was a good enough pitcher to keep anything from being hit to you."

"Come on, Mo, don't get nostalgic. We both know you were a great pitcher. I didn't mean to suggest that I could have done it without you. But all that's ancient history. We're not kids playing ball anymore."

"No, we're not."

"But, since you brought it up, I've been wanting to ask you, whatever happened to you, with baseball, I mean? You never talk about it. Why did you quit? You had everything."

Buttermaker scratched his head and closed his eyes. "I got tired. Tired of working so hard, tired of soaking my arm to get the pain out after every game I pitched, tired of losing, tired of having so many teammates depending on me, and letting them down."

"You didn't lose many, Mo. If you'd have kept going, you could have had a great career, a great life."

"I'm not complaining."

Whitewood smirked at him. "No, that's one thing you never do, complain. You just get tired."

Buttermaker shrugged. "I'm not sure these kids are tired yet."

Whitewood sighed impatiently. "But I am, Mo, and you are." He stood up and leaned forward across his desk. "Look, chum, it's been humiliating enough, for everybody. I went through an awful lot of trouble for this, arguing with the Council, then taking it to court, then talking you into coaching, spending a lot of money. And now it's time to—"

"You wouldn't want to throw good money after bad," said Buttermaker, smiling faintly, "isn't that it, Bob?" Whitewood started to speak, but Buttermaker held up his hand. "Okay, I'll tell them. But since you actually formed the team, maybe you could—"

Whitewood's secretary poked her head in the door. "Excuse me," she said, "but your two-thirty appointment, the farm-labor representative, is here."

"Send him in. Thanks, Mo, thanks for everything." Buttermaker nodded, turned, and walked out.

CHAPTER 4

Buttermaker stared through the new windshield of his car into the distance, at the Bears on the diamond. They were sitting on the ground, clustered around the pitcher's mound, fumbling with their mitts, a few chewing casually on blades of grass.

He drained his beer, got out, and walked over to them. They didn't look up, just sat silently. He squatted outside the circle of boys. "Okay, get it off your chests," he said. "I deserve whatever you have to say. Yell at me."

"We don't feel much like yelling, Coach," Jimmy Feldman said, "not at anybody. It's just that . . ." He bit his lip. Ogilvie nudged him to continue. "Well, we've been thinking about a few things, and, well, we've taken a lot of razzing in school. And most of us figure that you were probably right . . ." Tanner turned away in disgust and spat on the grass. "That we just weren't cut out to be ballplayers."

"That how you feel about it, Tanner?" Buttermaker asked.

Tanner turned toward him, his face puffy with bruises and adorned with three new Band-aids. "NO!"

"What happened to your face?" Buttermaker asked.

Tanner shook his head.

"Like Jimmy was saying," Regi Tower said, "we've taken a lot of teasing in school. Tanner doesn't go for that kind of stuff. He got into a fight."

"With who?"

"The seventh grade," Engelberg said, pulling at some blades of grass.

"So anyway," Jimmy said, "we took a vote and decided that we'd quit."

Ogilvie stood up and examined his score sheet. "The first game's statistics had something to do with our—the team's—decision. We committed thirteen errors in our only inning. Our pitcher gave up twelve hits, including five home runs. Inasmuch as we failed to make a single put-out, it is impossible to compute Lefty's earned-run average, since it would reach infinity." Lefty hung his head. "Similarly, since we did not come to bat, our batting average cannot be computed, except as nil. Altogether, our 21–0 defeat produced the vote to quit, by the margin of six to three, with two abstentions."

Buttermaker slowly scanned the group. "I should tell you," he said, "that some very important people have also suggested that we quit. You don't want to quit, Tanner?"

Tanner shook his head rapidly.

"Who else doesn't want to quit?"

"Jose an' me," Miguel said forcefully, "we vote PLAY!"

Buttermaker looked from one boy's bowed head to another's.

"I ain't quitting," came a soft voice from Toby Whitewood.

"But you voted . . ." Engelberg whined.

"I'm changing my vote. I ain't quitting, not after all my dad went through for this."

"Geez," Tanner said, spitting, "your dad!"

Toby sprang to his feet. "Well, I don't care what you think. We got a team from somewhere. And somebody's got to stand up for it!"

Tanner jumped up. "I been standing up for it all along!"

"Jose and me standing!" yelled Miguel as the brothers bounced to their feet.

"I never voted nohow," said Ahmad, joining them. "I'm ready for ACTION!"

"Neither did I cast a ballot," said Ogilvie, who remained standing. "But I am fully confident."

One by one the boys rose, until all were standing, looking down at Buttermaker, who remained on his haunches, studying the grass.

"You standin' too, Coach?" Ahmad asked.

Buttermaker rose wearily, closed his eyes, and sighed. "Yeah, I'm standing. Quitting is a bad habit, hard to break once you start."

"Yeah," Ahmad said, smiling broadly, "it's like you told me, Coach."

"So"—Buttermaker started pulling equipment out of the duffle bag—"I know I've been a lousy manager. You guys haven't played so hot either. But I guess we're stuck with each other."

"And remember this, Coach," Ogilvie said, as several Bears began happily grabbing up their gear, "we haven't actually been BEATEN by anybody yet."

"Right, Ogilvie, not yet."

As the rest took their positions, Engelberg and Lefty stayed next to Buttermaker. "I gotta tell you," Engelberg said, munching on a chocolate bar, "Lefty and me ain't too happy with this. We took a democratic vote to quit, and—"

Buttermaker slapped the candy bar out of his mouth and grabbed him harshly by the shoulders. "Listen, kid!" he shouted in a voice loud enough for the entire team to hear. "Nobody's vote counts around here except MINE! Now get your fat behind over to home plate before I KICK it there! Double for you, Lefty, I want that fast ball HUMMING!"

The two boys scampered into position. "Fascist," muttered Engelberg.

Buttermaker followed Lefty to the mound. "We got a game with the Athletics on Wednesday," he said, "and, Bears, that means only one thing: BAD NEWS for the ATHLETICS! Feldman, get up to the plate!"

Lefty pitched to Jimmy Feldman, who chopped a weak grounder to second, where Miguel knocked it down.

"Catch it, Miguel!" Buttermaker yelled. "Don't play with it! And, Feldman, you're dragging your right foot when you swing. PLANT it!"

Jimmy lined the next pitch to left.

Jose stepped into the batter's box. He swung nearly straight up at the pitch, missing it by a mile.

"Swing level," Buttermaker called. Jose wrinkled his brow questioningly. Buttermaker trotted up to the plate and guided him through a proper swing. On his next try he missed, but swung straight.

"Bueno, bueno!" called Buttermaker, clapping his hands.

For an hour, Bear after Bear swung at Lefty's pitches. The pitches came closer and closer to the plate, and the bats came closer and closer to the ball. Lefty was throwing harder, the Bears were swinging harder— missing most, but hitting some.

A ground ball went under Tanner's glove. Buttermaker took a fielder's stance next to him. "See, Tanner, I'm down low, with a leg behind the glove. Even if I miss the ball with my glove, my leg will stop it from going through to the outfield, and I can still make the play."

Tanner nodded. He began crouching lower for ground balls, and the other infielders copied him.

Finally Buttermaker yelled, "LAPS!" And he led the pack as they trotted around the fence. He began a loud chant: "A busted bat and a long fly ball . . ."

The panting Bears picked up the rhyme: "ANY DAY NOW DUROCHER WILL CALL!"

Ogilvie fell in beside Ahmad, puffing as he spoke. "I've read . . . everything about Hank Aaron, Ahmad . . . This forty-two-errors thing . . . is a . . . complete falsehood."

Ahmad stepped up his pace and pulled away in front.

Ogilvie dropped back with Engelberg, far to the rear. Then the two suddenly slipped through a hole in the fence. They flopped down on their backs, gasping for breath.

Engelberg clutched at his chest. "Person of my size . . . shouldn't . . . push himself . . . so hard," he said. "Heart attack . . . any minute now."

"I'll remember you well," said Ogilvie, gasping, "to your family."

Buttermaker's head appeared through the fence. "Fine! You both can spend the next two games on the bench!"

He trotted off, Engelberg scrambling through the fence in pursuit.

"It's not fair!" Engelberg yelled. "I can't be expected to run this much. I'll get a note from my psychiatrist, my pediatrician, my momma! I'm too fat to run!"

"Either you run," Buttermaker called back over his shoulder, "or you don't play."

Engelberg stopped short and put his hands on his hips. "FASCIST!" he screeched.

Tanner, at a full gallop, booted him in the rear. "Shut up your cruddy trap and MOVE, you blimp!"

Engelberg and Ogilvie stumbled after the team. "Conspiracy," Engelberg muttered, puffing, to Ogilvie, "minority rule!"

As the Bears trotted off the field, Roy Turner pulled his car up beside Buttermaker in the parking lot. He stepped out and angrily grabbed Buttermaker's elbow.

"What in blazes are you doing with these boys?" he sputtered.

"Getting ready for a game with the Athletics," said Buttermaker calmly. "Now get your arm off me, Turner."

Turner angrily slung his arm away. "Whitewood told me you were calling it quits," he said, his eyes blazing.

"We're not."

"You're crazy, Buttermaker. What in hell are you trying to do?"

"Win a pennant." Turner slapped his hands to his head. Buttermaker continued, pulling out a sheet of paper from his pocket. "This schedule says that on June nineteenth, the last day of the season, the two best teams will play for the title. I assume your Yankees will be one of those teams. We aim to be the other. If you'll excuse me . . ."

As Turner stared in speechless disbelief, Buttermaker got into his car and slammed the door. "See you on the field of play."

The Bears, despite their first-game humiliation, were excited for their second game. They huddled around Buttermaker just outside the dugout, their hands clasped together. "All right, guys," Buttermaker said, "I want some hard-nosed play out there. Now, once with feeling: First base, second base—"

"Aw," whined Toby, "do we have to do that corny—"

"I said with FEELING! First base, second base, third base, home . . ."

The Bears picked it up: "Around them bases we shall ROAM!"

But they didn't roam around the bases. They swung hard, but hit nothing except a few easy grounders and a handful of foul balls. They fielded hard, but the balls eluded them. Lefty threw hard, but the Athletics slammed his pitches all over the place.

Ahmad, wearing sunglasses in right field, almost caught two fly balls; Tanner, running all out and sliding desperately into first base on his belly, almost beat out a grounder; Engelberg, gritting his teeth, almost held on to the ball to tag a runner out at home.

At the end, the new scoreboard had the bad news: *Athletics—18, Bears—0.*

In the dugout following the game, Buttermaker paced back and forth before his dirty, glum team. "Lighten up, you guys," he said, "we finished the whole game, didn't we? Lots of close ones. Tanner almost got a single in the fourth—"

"I was SAFE! The ump's a crud."

"Okay, okay, we've improved. Rome wasn't built in a day."

"In fact," said Ogilvie, waving an index finger in the air, "it took several hundred years."

"Eighteen to nothing," muttered Lefty, "and to the worst team in the league."

"SECOND worst," grumbled Engelberg.

"Snap out of it, now!" Buttermaker barked. "Nobody said this would be easy."

"Easy," snarled Tanner, examining a few new scrapes on his elbows from diving attempts at ground balls, "it ain't."

"Well, on the brighter side," said Ogilvie, perusing the box score, "we committed only twenty-four errors in the entire game. And although their pitcher threw a no-hitter against us, we did manage to produce several foul balls, and even a couple fair."

Buttermaker chuckled and waved a ten-dollar bill. "Hot dogs and Cokes on me!" he yelled cheerfully. "Let's move!"

Whatever optimism had been generated by the few foul balls and couple of close plays in the 18–0 loss to the Athletics dissipated quickly in the sloppy practices and game that followed. The Bears lost their third straight, 13–1, to the Indians.

Briefly jubilant about scoring their first run of the season, the Bears' joy turned as fast to dismay, for it had been a costly score.

Lefty Stein was awarded first base after being hit by a pitch. He went to second when he mistakenly thought a pitch to Tanner was ball four, when in fact it was ball three, but luckily went in safely when the catcher's throw to second was wild. He went to third when Ahmad bunted, although Ahmad was thrown out at first. And he went home on a wild pitch—though not right away.

The pitch had skidded under the catcher and rolled back into the grass beyond the backstop. Buttermaker screamed for Lefty to come home, but Lefty just hopped up and down on the third-base bag, uncertain of what to do. The catcher searched madly for the ball, finally hollering out: "I can't find it!"

At that, Lefty finally broke for the plate, went into a wild, tumbling, totally unnecessary slide, and scored, with the Bears cheering tumultuously.

They all ran out to embrace their pitcher, but Lefty got up slowly, his face contorted in pain. He was holding his right wrist, which was already swelling.

The circle of Bears stepped back in stunned silence as Buttermaker ran up and put his arm around Lefty. He took the pitcher's damaged wrist in his fingers and lightly explored the bone with quick, deft movements.

"It's okay," Buttermaker said, "not broken, but sprained. You'll have to rest it awhile, but it'll be okay."

Lefty smiled wanly, holding his wrist, and the Bears, happy but now subdued, trotted together back to the dugout, where Buttermaker immersed the inflated joint in ice.

So the Bears had scored a run, and they had also managed, in their third game, to get their first two infield hits. Things were getting better, but not much. At this rate of improvement, they would still end with a clean 0–15 slate.

And now their pitcher was hurt. If Buttermaker had been willing to quit after the opening game, he was more than willing after the third. Losing made him tired.

He sat in his Cadillac in the league parking lot. A half-moon bathed the empty field in dim light. He drank slowly from his whiskey-and-beer mix. He felt lonely. He had felt lonely for so many years. He wondered if any of the Bears felt lonely. He guessed they didn't, because they all had homes to go to with other people in them.

Buttermaker sighed. People. He would love to quit this baseball garbage and just go on cleaning swimming pools. One thing about pools: Nobody was around when you cleaned them.

If it were up to him alone, he would quit coaching. He had quit before when a team needed him. But they had been pros, and he had been one of them. These were kids, and he was not one of them, but responsible. If he quit, the whole team would die. So he was forced NOT to quit.

"Quit or lose," he muttered, "what a choice."

But since he couldn't quit, was he thereby actually forced to lose? Was the whole team condemned to lose forever?

"Damned if we will!" He exhaled harshly into the darkness, shaking his head. "I gotta do something."

But what? He had taught them as best he could, practiced them hard, never missing a day, and gotten them into condition. There wasn't a born ballplayer among them.

Meticulously he thought through every phase of the game, looking for a weakness that might magically be corrected. A couple of minor things occurred to him. He nodded. "Not much, but might help a little."

He took a long drink, trying to raise his spirits, which were harder and harder to lift as the days went by.

For every minor improvement he thought he might seek, a major problem appeared. For example, who could pitch? The only likely prospects were Tanner, and maybe Jimmy Feldman. But Tanner was the best player, sorely needed at shortstop. He was the only in-fielder who could reasonably be expected to capture a ground ball and throw a runner out. Feldman's arm was reasonably accurate, but there was nobody to replace him in left field, except Ogilvie or Lupus. "Geez!" as those two would be the first to say.

He took another long drink. The improvements he thought of weren't enough. He was scraping the bottom of the barrels of both talent and hope. He had to do everything possible to help this ridiculous team. It was personnel he needed, not maneuvers. What was left?

He shook his head. If only he weren't so blasted TIRED, so he could think more clearly. He snapped open another can of beer, and reached into the glove compartment for the whiskey. His hand brushed the crumpled-up letter, and he jumped as if stung by a bee.

He sat back and stared at the Jim Beam, and at the crumpled letter, both silhouetted by the tiny glove-compartment light. He closed his eyes and thought a bit.

"Well," he muttered aloud at last, "if I can't quit one thing, maybe I could quit another. It's a long shot, but then, so's life."

He took the whiskey and the three remaining cans of beer, got out of the car, walked over to the trash can, and dumped them in. The whiskey bottle smashed as it hit the bottom. The acrid smell of spilled alcohol filled his nostrils.

And then suddenly, as if borne on the fumes themselves, an idea wafted into his head. He snapped his eyes wide open and grinned. "Simple," he said, pounding his right fist into his left hand, "you need a pitcher, you get a pitcher. Maybe, just maybe . . ."

He laughed out loud. He looked up at the fading moon and raised a fist and called out joyfully: "Here come the Bears with some BAD NEWS!"

Adding softly, "I think."

* * *

Buttermaker was not the only one fighting depression over the Bears. In several homes around town, young boys were trying to deal with the steady pounding of their hopes. Originally these Bears had been ecstatic over the unexpected opportunity just to play baseball on an official league team. They certainly hadn't counted on winning all their games. But neither had they anticipated being trounced so woefully, so consistently. And they hadn't reckoned with being ridiculed.

Jimmy Feldman and his father sat in wicker chairs on their small back lawn, watching a puppy roll and tumble in the grass.

"I'm telling you, Dad," Jimmy said, "you just wouldn't BELIEVE how bad we are."

"So," his father said gently, "it's just a game. Don't worry about it. Losing games means nothing. Just have fun."

"It's not that, Dad. We don't have to win. We just have to be a little, you know, proud of ourselves. But we're ASHAMED. How can you have fun? We actually voted to quit."

"Be glad that you didn't quit."

"Yeah, I guess so." Jimmy reached down to roll the puppy over onto its back and scratch its pink belly. "I guess we'll just have to try and make the best of it. But sometimes I wish we HAD quit. What if we don't win a single game?"

"So"—his father hunched his shoulders and held his palms up—"you may NOT win a game. But then one day you will look back at all this and laugh."

Jimmy shook his head. "Maybe. But, to tell you the truth, right now I'd rather be in the stands laughing at US, than on the field being laughed AT. The people having all the fun are the guys playing against us. We're miserable."

"So"—his father chuckled—"maybe a little misery is good for you."

"It's great," Jimmy said, "just great."

Mike Engelberg shoved his supper aside, half eaten. "Mikey, eat," his mother pleaded with sad eyes.

"Naw, Ma, I gotta slim down. Our coach is a tyrant. A FASCIST! He makes us run ten miles a day. I can't keep up. He says I can't play if I don't run."

"You shouldn't run ten miles, my son," his father said. "You want I should talk to this coach? You want, I'll talk to him. Maybe you shouldn't play."

"I GOTTA play. They FORCE you to play. And besides, the whole team depends on me. I'm in a slump, so we're getting blown apart. I'm the only hope we got. Don't talk to the coach. I can handle him. He needs me."

"Eat, Mikey, please," his mother said, pushing his plate back in front of him. "For your mother, eat."

"Your mother says eat," his father said, "so eat. Catchers have to be strong."

"Aw, okay. But tomorrow I gotta slim down. You know what the Yankees call me? Lard-blossom. What a tough sport."

Ahmad Abdul Rahim's two older brothers alternated throwing the ball high into the evening sun. Ahmad drifted back and forth for the catches.

"Hey," he said, carefully watching the arc of the ball, "you know Hank Aaron got forty-two errors his first year?" The ball plopped into his glove.

"That right?" one brother said. "He's come a good way."

"Yeah, Coach said he decided never to quit trying."

"Well," said the other brother, flinging one to tree-top level, "that's one way you're just like ol' Hank."

The ball dropped through Ahmad's glove and bounced off his chest. "Yeah, and that's about the ONLIEST way," he said.

The two older brothers laughed.

"See," Ahmad said, pouting, "you're just like everybody else, laughin'."

"No we're not," the first brother said. "We're trying to help you get better."

"It ain't no use," said Ahmad, sitting down on the grass. "Ballplayers ain't taught, they're just born."

"Only things just born," said the second brother, sitting down beside him, "is babies."

"You got it, bro, that's what we are, baby Bears. Baby Bears gettin laughed at good and whupped bad by ballplayers."

"Well," said his brother, getting up, "since we don't want no crybaby Bears in our house, you better haul yourself on up and get ready to catch some more fly balls. Come on."

"Aw, only thing I'm good for is a clown."

"Fine. If that's your act, then we gonna get that act together. You gonna be a clown that can catch fly balls. Come on."

"Don't laugh no more."

"Nope. As a clown, you ain't all that funny."

The three of them laughed.

"Are you ashamed of us, Dad?"

Councilman Whitewood looked up from the sheaf of documents he was studying. "Of course not, why?"

"Well, we're doing so bad, after all you did to get us

a team. And you don't come around to practices any more."

His father cleared his throat. "Oh, that's just because I'm so busy, Toby."

"Did you know that most of the guys voted to quit after the first game?"

"I heard about it. Under the circumstances, it might not have been such a bad idea to admit that maybe you just weren't quite ready to—"

"I refused to quit," Toby said. "A couple of others did too—Tanner, Miguel, Jose . . ."

"Coach Buttermaker talk you out of quitting, by any chance?"

"No, SIR! He didn't say much at all, just asked us how we felt." Toby scuffed his feet on the thick shag carpet. "I don't think he wanted us to quit, though."

"What makes you think that?"

"Well, none of us are HIS sons, you know, so why the heck would he be out there every day coaching us, unless he wanted us to stick it out?"

"Maybe he just doesn't care that much about it, whether you win or lose," his father said, leafing through some documents.

"He's GOTTA care. We're not just winning or losing, we're a JOKE. Nobody wants to be a dumb joke."

"So why keep playing?"

"Well, because we're already a joke. If we stop playing now, we'll be a joke forever. The only chance we got is to become a real baseball team."

"Not much of a chance of that, is there?"

"Not much, but that's all we got."

Lefty Stein had worked up a sweat, from both exertion and pain. He stood in the bathroom, dressed only in underpants, practicing his wind-up in front of the full-length mirror on the door. Every time he swung his arm, his wrist hurt, even though he had it tightly wrapped with an Ace bandage. He figured he might have to miss the next game. But when he COULD pitch again, he intended to have the smoothest, strongest delivery in the league.

He wound up again, and winced.

There was an insistent knock. "Come on, Lefty, you weirdo, you been in there twenty minutes!"

"Beat it, brat. I'll be out when I'm ready. What a sister!" He went into his motion again, watching his reflection closely, his tongue pressed between his teeth in concentration.

Another knock. "What are you DOING in there, anyway, all the live-long day?"

"I'm THINKING, mudball!"

"Thinking about WHAT, scarecrow, your beloved BEARS?"

"Yes, twerp, about my beloved BEARS!"

"Then I guess"—she giggled loudly—"the bathroom is just the place for it."

Lefty swore under his breath.

She knocked again. "Come on, bean-brain, Mommy says it's my turn, and Daddy says you gotta be fair."

"Oh, for PETE'S SAKE!" Lefty massaged his wrist. "Nothing in my life is fair." He took one last windup, put on his bathrobe, hid the glove under it, unlocked the door, and stomped out, shoving his little sister aside.

Regi Tower's father shook his head. "You've got another spot of gravy on your shirt, Regi. Can't we take you ANYWHERE to eat?"

"We could have just stayed home then," Regi said, pouting.

"Yeah, that would be the EASY thing to do,

wouldn't it? Rather than improving your eating habits. Just like it would be easier to stay home than to attack those grounders at third base."

Regi's mother patted his father's arm and clucked her tongue softly. "There, there, George, let's leave Regi alone tonight. He has enough problems, in school, playing baseball, trying to make friends. Let's just enjoy our dinner." She smiled in a very motherly way at Regi.

"He's gotta get some backbone, Ethel," his father said, scowling, and stabbing a piece of steak with his fork. "You can see that on the baseball field. All those boys on his team need some backbone. They're letting everybody DESTROY them out there. It's time—"

"You think that's EASY?" Regi snapped, tears flooding his eyes. "You think it's EASY to keep going out there when you know how bad it's gonna be every time? YOU THINK THAT'S EASY?"

"Shut up, Regi," his father whispered, glancing nervously around the restaurant.

Mr. Agilar sat reading a Spanish-language newspaper and smoking his pipe. Mrs. Agilar knitted on the far side of the room. Their two daughters could be heard arguing mildly in the kitchen.

Jose and Miguel alternated spinning the arrow on a baseball game on the frayed living-room rug.

Mr. Agilar spoke in Spanish: "Baseball, baseball, baseball." He chuckled and shook his head as he turned a page. "That's all you boys think about."

"It's FUN," Jose said.

"Even more fun here," Miguel added, "than on the field with a real team of your own, because here you can WIN."

Mr. Agilar chuckled again and tamped down the

ashes of his pipe with his thumb. "Think what it would be like to win a real game with your real team."

"Oh, we'll win," Jose said, "maybe."

"At least we have a team," Miguel said, "that's the important thing."

"Well," Mrs. Agilar said, nodding, "it's very lucky you have a team. Quite a man, that Mr. Whitewood."

"Not as good as Coach Buttermaker," Miguel said.

"Except that," Jose said, "he likes to sleep a lot."

He and Miguel looked at each other and giggled.

Mr. Agilar leaned down toward them. "I have a feeling about your Coach Buttermaker. I've been watching him, and I think maybe he's not as sleepy as you think. I think he would try to make you a GOOD team."

"I wouldn't mind," Jose said.

"But if we had a good team," Miguel said, spinning the dial, "then Jose and I wouldn't be playing."

Timmy Lupus and his mother stood on a downtown street corner, framed by the light from a street lamp as they waited for the bus.

"Are you enjoying yourself, Timmy," she asked him, "playing baseball with the other boys?"

"Uh-hunh."

"Does everybody get along with . . . with everybody else?"

"Uh-hunh."

She leaned out to look up the street for the tardy bus. "I wish I didn't have to work the hours I do, so I could see you play. Would you like for me to see you play?"

"Uh-hunh."

"Is there, uh, anything you need, you know, do you have what the other boys have, a good-enough mitt and all?"

Timmy scuffed his feet on the sidewalk and kicked a

stone into the gutter. "Something I would like, but . . . not something you have to buy."

"Just tell me."

He looked up at his mother. "What I would like most is . . ." He looked away.

"Go ahead."

"Is, if I could stop going to Dr. Freulich, maybe, just for a while, like just for the rest of the games, because . . ."

"Timmy, tell me exactly how you feel, go ahead."

" 'Cause"—he began to speak rapidly—"it just makes me feel so DIFFERENT. Like there's something WRONG with me, and the other boys know it, and they laugh." He looked up at her hopefully.

She smiled. "Okay. Dr. Freulich just helped you understand yourself a little better. Everybody needs that sometimes. Even your teammates. But you're ahead of them. So we'll say that today was our last visit with Dr. Freulich. Okay?"

Timmy smiled, and they hugged each other. "You know what?" he said. "Coach Buttermaker says that if we improve about five hundred percent, we might WIN a game pretty soon."

"And I'll be watching," she said, "I really will."

"The so-called law of averages," Ogilvie's father said to him as they peered at each other through their thick spectacles, "is not a natural law, such as that governing the pendulum, but merely a conjecture, based on our belief in the natural balance of nature."

"Be that as it may," said Ogilvie, his index finger high, "the law of averages is what we base optimism and pessimism on. Therefore, the Yankees, who have won four straight North Valley League championships, must fear the law of averages, and thus be pessimistic.

While the Bears, on the other hand, may as well be optimistic. For not only have we never won a title, but we have not even won a game. So in the natural course of events . . ."

His father waved his hand. "I'm afraid I don't know much about baseball."

"But the point is," Ogilvie went on, "the same forces govern baseball as govern, say, insurance, with which you are more familiar. The basic rule of your insurance business is that, regardless of specific setbacks to the company, such as a few large unexpected claims, in time things will even out, leaving a profit for the company."

"But, my son," his father said, raising an index finger, "in insurance we have statistics, showing curves and tendencies."

"AHA!" answered Ogilvie, waving his finger. "So do WE. The Bears have improved their performance with each passing game, as shown by the actual scores. We have cut the runs-against by roughly fifty percent since the first game. Projecting that tendency upon the rest of the season—"

"Excuse me, my boy, not to change the subject, but do you ever actually PLAY in a game?"

"Of course. But I am not, as you well know, an athlete. I consider my primary role to be that of statistician. It is through statistics that I am able to most help the team, to demonstrate our expectations and to promote encouragement among the players by showing our statistical improvement."

"Well." His father took off his glasses to polish them. "I can only hope that you are good at it."

"I am, if I may say, excellent. And you will see, at the close of our season, that my statistics were not only accurate, but prophetic." He paused a moment. "Even though the hilarity which currently greets our team at each game might, to the shortsighted, suggest otherwise."

Tanner Boyle sat on the metal kitchen chair, sharing a sandwich with a black mutt that resembled a terrier.

He heard the door slam. "Ma?"

There was no answer. His older sister appeared in the kitchen doorway.

"Where's Ma?" Tanner asked, taking a bite of sandwich.

"Out."

"She gonna be home later?"

"Who knows? None of your business, anyway."

"Geez. Nothing for supper, either."

"Looks to me like you're EATING supper."

Tanner tossed the remains of the sandwich on the table top in disgust. "Old baloney and one measly slice of bread. You call that supper?"

His sister tossed her black hair and shrugged her shoulders.

Tanner picked up the last bit of sandwich and stuffed it into his mouth. He chewed and swallowed it quickly. "Well, what are YOU gonna eat for supper?"

"Somebody's bringing me pizza. You wanna eat out?"

"I ain't got a dime," Tanner said.

"I'll give you a dollar."

Tanner looked up.

"But on one condition."

"Yeah, I know . . ."

"Don't come back before ten."

"Geez! Can't even stay in my own house! Hey, does it ever occur to you that I'm tired, worn out? I practice baseball TWO HOURS every day."

"Yeah," she said in a snide voice, "I and all my friends have enjoyed reading about that in the paper. What a team you've got."

Tanner stiffened. "What do you mean by that?"

"Sounds like a bunch of MONKEYS could beat your BEARS."

Tanner sprang up, his fists clenched.

His sister stepped backward, smiling, and waved a dollar bill at him. "You want this," she teased, "or not?"

Tanner snatched the dollar from her hand and stalked toward the door. "Geez! If I didn't have to EAT . . ." He slammed the door behind him.

CHAPTER 5

"You want us to SPY, Coach?" Engelberg said, his eyes opened wide in surprise.

"Not spy," Buttermaker said, "scout. Scouting is not spying. It's entirely legal. All it means is that you watch other teams play, and take notes on the things I tell you to look for. Scouting is one of the most important tools of a winning ball club. It helps us know what to expect from other teams, what pitches certain players like to swing at, what their weaknesses are."

"Geez, I don't know," Engelberg said, shaking his head slowly and looking out at the diamond, where the Bears were throwing the ball around prior to practice. "It sounds scary."

Buttermaker sighed and dropped his arm off Engelberg's shoulder. "Tell him, Ogilvie," he said, "tell him scouting is okay."

"He's right, Engelberg," Ogilvie said, adjusting the glasses on his nose. "Scouting opposing teams is a perfectly acceptable and normal activity. All the professional teams in every sport engage in the activity of—"

"Hey, Ogilvie," Engelberg said, "I KNOW that. I KNOW about sports. I just didn't think that, uh, teams did it in, uh, this league."

"Maybe other teams don't," Buttermaker said. He squatted down and put a hand on a shoulder of each boy. "But it's not because they're not supposed to. Maybe they haven't thought of it. Maybe they're not as smart as we are. Maybe they've got more experienced players, and they don't think they need to scout. But we've got to do everything possible to have a chance at the championship."

"Coach Buttermaker," Ogilvie said, raising a finger, "aren't you getting things a little out of perspective here? It's one thing to improve"—he glanced down at his handful of statistics sheets—"but quite another thing to start talking of a championship."

"And the Yankees have won the last four pennants in a row," Engelberg said. "I don't see Mr. Turner sending anybody around to scout US. So why—"

"You don't see his SCOUTS?" Buttermaker leaned back and put his hand on his forehead. "What do you think his son, Joey, is doing at our practices, at our games? Just why do you think he's always around when—"

"He's laughing, mostly," Engelberg said, pouting.

"That's just a cover-up," Buttermaker said, "for his real mission. He is SCOUTING us."

"You think so?" Engelberg said.

"I should think," Ogilvie said, "that there would be no need to scout us for weaknesses. Our weaknesses are all too apparent. For example—"

"I don't need to hear your examples," said Buttermaker, lightly swatting Ogilvie's finger away from his face. "Take it from me, the Yankees are worried about us. And you know why? Because we're BAD NEWS for the Yankees."

"I still think any talk about a championship is—"

"Shut up and let me worry about that. We play one game at a time. Now, back to scouting. The White Sox play the Mets tomorrow at four o'clock. We play the Mets on Thursday. You two be at their game tomorrow. I want a full report on their hitters."

Ogilvie nodded.

Engelberg snapped up straight, his chest out, his face stern. "Is that an order?"

"That's an order, Engelberg."

"Geez!"

Buttermaker drove slowly, searching the sidewalk with his eyes as he maneuvered his Cadillac around the Hollywood side streets. He sped up slightly as he spotted a small, hand-written sign in the distance: GUIDES TO MOVIE STARS' HOMES. As he approached, he saw a small boy clutching maps in one hand and waving down passing cars with the other.

Buttermaker shook his head and continued on. Another sign caught his eye, and he turned the car toward it. An old woman wearing a wide-brimmed hat was sitting motionless on a stool next to the sign. He frowned and drove on.

He turned the corner by a movie marquee. A woman waved to him. It was Jill Turner. He pulled the car over and stopped. Mrs. Turner opened the passenger door and slid in.

"Hi," she said cheerfully.

"Hi," he said. "Uh, where you headed?"

"Anywhere." She smiled at him.

"I'm just, uh, kind of driving around the neighborhood," he said.

"Fine."

"Well." Buttermaker tapped the steering wheel nervously. "How're things?"

"Just like they always are," she said, "with me, at least. Your Bears are really taking it on the chin."

Buttermaker chuckled as he drove slowly along, no longer looking at the sidewalk. "Yeah, they sure are. WE sure are. But we're hanging in, for whatever that's worth. Your Yankees are sure burning up the league."

"Not MY Yankees," she said, "ROY'S Yankees. Yeah, they are always on top. They've got a man who considers himself a great coach."

Buttermaker raised his eyebrows and looked at her. "You don't think he's a great coach?"

She shrugged and stared straight ahead. "Well, I think that once you've won a championship, you kind of get the pick of the boys from then on. And then if you pound into the boys that the most important thing in their lives is winning baseball games, then I guess you win baseball games. But I must say, he's kind of a depressing guy to live—"

"Let's talk about something else," Buttermaker said quickly.

"Okay."

They rode a few minutes in silence.

"I think winning is important," Buttermaker said.

"I thought you wanted to talk about something else."

"Yeah."

"Why don't you come by the house some day?" she said.

He looked at her. "I work during the day, just like Roy does."

"Well," she said, smiling, "you could clean our pool."

"Sure," he said, without smiling back. "Well, I have

100

an appointment, so if you could just tell me where I could drop you . . ."

"Here is fine. Give me a call."

"Sure."

He watched her close the door, waved, and drove off, again scanning the sidewalks.

He headed into a neighborhood of lush greenery and big homes. He made a right turn near another small sign advertising movie-star maps. A car with Georgia license plates was just pulling away from the curb near where a small girl with shoulder-length blond hair, wearing dungarees and a T-shirt, sat in a black director's chair reading a glamor magazine.

He parked and got out. He walked casually over to the girl. She was deeply absorbed in her magazine. Buttermaker snapped his fingers, and she looked up.

Her mouth fell open in surprise. Buttermaker smiled. "Nice corner you've got here, Amanda. Really coming up in the world."

She regained her composure and smiled wryly. "Long time no see, suds-head. How's the chlorine pouring?"

Buttermaker sat down in the grass next to her as she returned to her magazine.

"I've been wondering how things were going, Amanda," he said.

"Have you?"

"Doing any pitching?"

"Yeah, I pitched a no-hitter for the Tigers in the World Series, didn't you read about it?"

Buttermaker chuckled and ripped up a few blades of grass. "If you can manage to be serious," he said, "can you still throw a curve ball?"

"Of course." She flipped through a few pages.

"Would you like to pitch for the North Valley League Bears?"

Amanda dropped her magazine and stared at him open-mouthed. "Are you kidding?"

"Nope."

"You gotta be kidding. A girl pitching in that league? You gotta be full of—"

"Girls are allowed now. One or two have played before. And we need a pitcher."

"No girl ever pitched in that league, so don't lie to me. A couple tried out and didn't make the teams. And anyway"—she snatched up her magazine and pretended to read—"I'm through with all that tomboy stuff. My sister says you almost ruined me with all that sports jazz."

"How is Brenda?"

"What's it to you?"

Buttermaker stared into the distance. "You developed yourself a pretty good curve ball once," he said thoughtfully. "I know. I watched you one day, at the park, pitching to some guy. So I know you kept it up."

She grunted.

"You afraid to play on a team?"

"You know I'm not afraid of anything."

"Then maybe you owe me something. I was kind of like a father to you."

"HA! Some father!"

"Didn't I take you horseback riding on Sundays?"

She stared into her magazine.

"Didn't I take you to the movies every week? Didn't I get you a math tutor?"

She whirled toward him and threw down her magazine. "Math tutor! He hadn't even finished high school himself. I got a D in math last year!"

"Well, then the guy lied to me," Buttermaker said grumpily, looking at the grass.

"Humph!"

Suddenly Buttermaker jumped up, smiling and waggling a finger at her. "Your APPENDIX! Hunh? How about that? Everybody thought you just had a stomachache. But I threw you into the car and got you to the hospital. How about that? You wouldn't be alive today if it weren't for me!"

She frowned and turned away.

"Well, don't you owe me something for that?"

A motorcycle roared up to the curb and stopped. "That dude botherin' you, babe?" the rider called.

"Naw." Amanda waved him away. "It's all right. He's a . . . he's an old friend."

Buttermaker walked over to the motorcyclist and stuck out his hand. "You're Kelly Leak," he said with a friendly smile. "I don't think we've been introduced. I'm—"

"I know who you are," Kelly said, revving his engine and moving away slowly. "Amanda, I'll be around the corner, if you need me."

Buttermaker walked back to Amanda. "Strange guy," he said.

"What's so strange?"

"Nothing, I guess. He hangs around the field quite a bit."

"So? Is that against the law?"

"No, no. Amanda, Brenda's okay? I think about her—"

"Look, Buttermaker. You spent a lot of time hanging around our place drunk. That's your business. You taught me how to throw a curve, that's fine. I can throw a beauty. But then one day you just up and walked out. My sister was sick about it. She wanted to marry you. What you do is your business, but when you hurt my sister, it's mine. She was dumb. I'm not. So I wish you'd just bug off and—"

"Your sister and I were very close, Amanda. Maybe we still are, or could be. I handled things badly."

"You handled things like a—" Buttermaker clapped his hand over her mouth. She spun her head away.

"You saving any money from this cute little job you got here?" he asked.

"Sure. And it ain't CUTE. It's a big business this time of year."

"What are you going to do with your money?"

"Well . . ." She pulled back her lips with a finger to bare her teeth. "I'm going to get some braces. And pretty soon I'm going to take ballet lessons, when I save up. And I'm going to be a model one day and make some really BIG bread."

Buttermaker nodded. "All right. Come and play ball. I'll pay for the ballet lessons. Braces might take a little time, because that's a lot of—"

"DARN IT! You miss the point of everything. I'm not going to mess myself up playing—"

"These boys don't play so rough, Amanda. You won't get hurt."

"That's got nothing to do with it! I'm almost twelve. Pretty soon I'll be wearing a—" She stopped, looked down at her flat body. "I can't be playing no dumb baseball," she said shyly.

Buttermaker stood up and smiled down at her. "Yeah, sorry, I guess you're right. I mean, about being a girl. I would forget this modeling thing, though. That's for jerks. Acting, that's for you. With the face you've got, and the poise. Acting. Shoot for that."

Amanda blushed and looked at her feet.

Buttermaker sighed. "And I suppose you wouldn't really have helped the team that much, because, bad as we are, we need somebody really TERRIFIC. You were great when you were nine. But girls reach their athletic peak at about that age."

She looked up at him and narrowed her eyes. "What do you mean by that?"

"Oh, you know, when girls get to be your age, nearing womanhood, they get a little gangly, awkward. And my experience is that their pitching arm begins to get a little soft."

He bent down and kissed the top of her head. She slapped his hand away and scowled. "Just what are you talking about? What do you mean about the pitching arm?"

"Just agreeing with you, my dear little Amanda. You're past your tomboy days and moving on to womanhood. Well"—he turned and started walking toward his car—"give my best to your sister. And I'll see you around."

"HOLD IT, SUDS-HEAD!" He turned back to her. She stood facing him, legs planted apart, arms folded across her chest. "I got my curve ball breaking two and a half feet! And my spitter moves like a snake!"

He cocked his head. "Spitter? I never taught you how to throw a spitter."

"No, but you TOLD me how. I practiced. But my curve ball is best."

"Okay, okay, so your curve ball is your best pitch. Fine. It was mine too. But don't go giving me that baloney about an eleven-year-old girl breaking off two-and-a-half-foot curves. That's not likely."

Amanda stomped quickly over to him and peered angrily up into his face. "You got five bucks that says I can't?"

He turned, opened the car door, reached in, and

pulled out two gloves and a ball. He tossed the ball and a glove to her. "I got ten."

She snatched the glove and ball out of the air, turned, and stomped the other way, stopping about forty feet from him.

He crouched down in a catcher's stance, pounding a fist in his glove and holding it up as a target. "Okay, girl, fire one in here."

Amanda wound up quickly and threw. It was a blazing fast ball that slammed into Buttermaker's glove. "Hey," he said, taking his glove off and rubbing his hand, trying to conceal his amazement over her speed, "I thought you were going to throw curves."

"You said fire, buster, so I fired. That was just to loosen up. Okay, watch it now. The bottom's gonna drop right out of this next one."

Just then a car squealed to a stop right behind Buttermaker's. It was the car with the Georgia plates. A man in a flowered shirt and golf hat and white shoes stepped out and walked quickly over to Amanda, waving his hand at her. "Hey, hey there, hey, little girl," he called with a broad drawl. "This here map you sold me for two dollars don't even have Liberace's house on it! We come all this way just to see Liberace's house! Now this here map cost me two dollars, and—"

Amanda arched her back and tilted her head skyward and closed her eyes and bellowed: "Blow it out your tailpipe, buster! I don't care how far you came! This is California! Go to the beach! Liberace moved to Pennsylvania! Now BEAT IT!"

The man stumbled backward, turned, jumped into his car, and sped away.

Buttermaker frowned a little at Amanda's coarseness. But she was already into her windup. He crouched down just in time to see a curve ball head for his eyes, then break off sharply and bounce off his right foot. He danced around on his left leg, trying to shake the pain off his other foot.

Amanda lay back her head and roared with laughter. "That curve just cost you ten bucks, old friend! Now get outta here and let me make a living, before my boyfriend comes back and knocks you on your can!" She lowered her voice a bit as she saw Buttermaker grinning at her. "And don't get your hopes up. I still don't know if I'll pitch for you or not. I'll think about it."

Kelly Leak got off his motorcycle and put his arm around Amanda.

"You didn't have to butt in, Kelly," she said sulkily.

"I just didn't like that guy messing with you, getting you upset," he said.

"Look, buster." Amanda pushed his arm off her shoulder. "I can take care of myself!"

"Hey, I know that," he said, holding his palms up in front of him. "I just wanted to remind you that I'm around, you know, when I'm needed."

They walked a few steps together.

"Hey, babe," he said, "you're not gonna go for all that baseball crap, are you?"

"I don't know." She spun to face him, her hands on her hips. "But why NOT? Who are you to call it crap? You hang around there enough!"

He hung his head and scuffed the dirt. "Aw, just for laughs. They're a bunch of babies. And besides, they're . . ." He cleared his throat. "They're . . ."

"Yeah?"

"They're boys," he said softly.

"Oh yeah? Well, I can hack it. I don't remember YOU being able to hit my curve ball."

"Aw, I wasn't really trying."

"Oh yeah? Well, maybe I need to try it out on some other guys who will try harder. Maybe you just made up my mind for me. Here." She handed him a bunch of movie-star maps and shoved him down into her chair. "You mind the store."

He stared after her as she walked away. "Where you goin'?"

"To the movies. To be an ACTRESS!"

Ogilvie and Engelberg stood a few feet behind the backstop, in a direct line of vision to the batter and pitcher. Engelberg chewed a sandwich. Ogilvie made notes on a clipboard.

A Met batter swung and missed.

"What was it, what was it?" Ogilvie whispered.

"Fash bahr, haraware."

"What? Will you please get that food out of your mouth."

Engelberg swallowed hard. "Sorry. Fast ball, high and away. Want a bite?"

"What is it?"

"Chicken salad, orange marmalade, and anchovies on whole wheat."

"Yuk. We got to keep an eye on the signals from the third-base coach too, don't forget."

The batter popped up weakly.

"Same pitch," Engelberg said, "high and outside."

"Got it."

The next batter was announced over the public-address system: "Now batting, the pitcher, Carl Karansky."

A rugged-looking, handsome Met swaggered up to the plate, drawing oohs and aahs from several admiring small girls. He lashed the first pitch against the left-field fence, and ended up on third with a triple.

"What'd he swing at, what'd he swing at?" whispered Ogilvie urgently.

"How the heck do I know? He HIT it."

Ogilvie shook his head. "How the devil are we going to pitch to Cool Carl Karansky?"

"Geez, I don't know. He ain't got no weakness."

Suddenly Ogilvie leaned forward intently and peered down the third-base line at the Met coach, who was moving his hands around rapidly, touching his cap, his chest, his pants. "Hey, look," he whispered, "look! That's a signal! They're gonna do something!"

The Met batter squared around to bunt, and as the pitcher threw, Karansky broke for the plate.

"A squeeze! The old squeeze play!"

Karansky slid safely across the plate as the confused catcher fielded the bunt, started to dive for Karansky, then started to throw to first, and ended up doing nothing.

"Write it down, write it down!" whispered Engelberg.

"Just keep your eyes on the field. I'm doing MY job," Ogilvie whispered back.

Buttermaker sat with Amanda in his Cadillac, looking out at the Bears scampering around the field, getting ready for practice. They both made notes on pads of paper as they spoke.

"Twelve ballet lessons," Amanda said.

"Nine lessons," he said.

"Twelve lessons or it's no go, suds-head."

"Come on, those things cost six bucks a shot."

"And for every shutout I throw, I want a pair of new jeans."

"Aw, for crying out loud."

"Imported jeans. As a matter of fact, I want French jeans."

"What's the matter with American jeans?"

"I want the most expensive kind."

"You know how many pools I got to clean to do this?"

"You ain't getting away cheap, buster, not on this."

"Hey, Amanda," he said, shaking his head and making another note on his pad, "who are you, Catfish Hunter?"

Back and forth they went. Finally, their negotiations concluded, they left the car and walked over to the diamond. Buttermaker chomped uneasily on his Tiparillo. Amanda followed him shyly a step behind.

He called the team in, and they gathered around, all eyes on Amanda.

"Boys," he said soberly, "you might as well know the truth. Lefty Stein won't be able to pitch anymore with that wrist."

Lefty, his wrist encased in the Ace bandage, stared at the ground.

"He'll be useful in other ways, but not as a pitcher. And so," he smiled expansively, "boys, meet your new pitcher, Amanda Whurlizer!"

The boys stared at Amanda, then at one another.

Tanner spit on the grass. "Jerks, foreigners, sissies, nose-pickers—and now, a GIRL!"

Amanda's head snapped up, and she took a step toward Tanner, her eyes afire. "Grab a bat, punk!"

Tanner glared at her.

"Go ahead, Tanner," Buttermaker said. "We might as well see what she can do right away."

Tanner spat and snapped up a bat, muttering to himself. Amanda trotted out to the pitcher's mound, and Tanner set himself at the plate.

She wound up and fired a fast ball. Tanner swung savagely as the pitch slammed into Engelberg's mitt.

"Ow!" Engelberg said. He shook the mitt off and blew on his hand. He looked over at Buttermaker. "Maybe you should catch these, Coach," he said, "just so you can watch better."

"Go ahead, Engelberg, you're going to have to catch her from now on."

"Geez!"

Amanda broke off a slow curve, and Tanner swung so hard that he fell down, facing the backstop. He got up slowly and spat. "Not too bad," he muttered, "for a broad."

Amanda quickly established herself with the boys. Although they were embarrassed at the idea of having a girl pitch for them, they were excited at the prospect of watching her sail those pitches past opposing batters—especially Yankees.

The practice sessions were marked by a renewed diligence and zest.

Buttermaker was excited too, although he wasn't as awed by Amanda as the others were. The best chance, he knew, was for Amanda to strike out everybody, since anybody who didn't strike out would more than likely get on base, so ragged was the Bears' fielding.

But he also knew that, good as Amanda was, she wasn't going to strike out everybody. Some batters were bound to get pieces of her fast balls. Her curve was something else—nobody would touch that. But she couldn't throw a curve on every pitch; her arm wouldn't last a week. And the spitter? Forget that. Illegal, immoral, impossible. An eleven-year-old couldn't throw a spitter, much less cleverly conceal the goo to put on the ball.

Buttermaker recalled with a chuckle his own abilities with the spitter. He had used it off-and-on his last season, then discarded it, not so much for its illegality as for the fact that it was a cop-out, an admission that he didn't have good-enough stuff anymore.

And besides whatever Amanda could do, the Bears, who had managed just two base hits in three games, didn't seem capable of producing enough runs to win, regardless of how good their pitching was.

So other aspects of the game had to be attended to. They were to face the Mets the next day. As the team practiced, Buttermaker sat in the dugout with Ogilvie, who pored over a thick manuscript on his lap.

"The Mets' leadoff batter is Bernard Sepcowiscz," Ogilvie said seriously. "Also known as Bernie, also known as Mushie. Born January 8, 1964. Sign is Capricorn. Mother and father divorced—"

"For Pete's sake, Ogilvie!" Buttermaker interrupted. "I don't want the guy's life story."

Ogilvie sniffed haughtily. "When I'm given an assignment, I like to do the most thorough job possible."

Buttermaker groaned and closed his eyes. "All I want to know is, does he hit inside, does he hit outside, does he like pitches high or low."

Ogilvie sighed, miffed that his talents were unappreciated, but used to it. "All right. He likes them high and away. He's a sucker for inside stuff. Usually hits to the opposite side of the field, which would be in this case, since he's a right-handed batter, our right field. Of course, that might present us with a slight problem, since our talents in right field have been noticeably lacking for—"

"Good," Buttermaker said. "Next?"

Ogilvie quickly rattled off the strengths and weaknesses of the next two hitters, then drew a deep breath.

"Which brings us to their cleanup batter, Carl Karansky. He is known to us as Cool Carl, because of his general—"

"Ogilvie, would you please just tell me what he hits and doesn't hit?"

"Well, the truth is"—Ogilvie shook his head mournfully—"he hits everything."

"Everything?"

"Yes. High, low, inside, outside, fast, slow. I would say"—he looked at Buttermaker with the confidence of an expert—"that outside of perhaps Joey Turner of the Yankees, whom I have not yet officially scouted, Cool Carl is the best hitter I have ever seen in my entire life."

"Mmm," Buttermaker said.

"In fact," Ogilvie continued, waving his index finger, "in the six times I saw him come to the plate, he hit two over the left-field fence, two against it on the fly, and two against it on a roll."

"Mmm." Buttermaker stared into the distance and scratched his head. "All to left field?"

"Yes. A tremendous pull-hitter."

"Mmm."

Amanda had been lobbing up easy ones for batting practice, and Feldman got a hold of one for a long foul to right. The ball rolled past the end of the fence and into the parking lot. Buttermaker tossed another old ball out to Amanda, and was about to send Lefty Stein after the foul ball when he saw Kelly Leak get off his motorcycle and head toward it casually.

Kelly picked up the ball just as Pigtails drove into the lot. She poked her head out the window. "Thought I told you to quit hanging around here, Kelly," she said gruffly.

Kelly shrugged, turned, and almost effortlessly threw a perfect strike all the way to home plate. Then he took out a cigarette, lit it, nodded to Pigtails, hopped onto his Harley, and sped away.

Buttermaker watched the course of the beautiful throw with his mouth hanging open. "What an arm!" He trotted out toward the mound, looking after the disappearing Kelly. The Bears gathered around him and Amanda.

"Wow!" he said. "Did you guys see that?"

The Bears looked at one another nervously, silently.

"Hey, that kid should be playing ball," Buttermaker said. "Hunh? What's the matter? Why isn't that kid playing? Is he too old, or what?"

Finally Toby spoke up. "He's not too old, Coach. And he's the best athlete in the area. But . . ."

"But he's Kelly Leak," Tanner said.

"Yeah, that's Kelly Leak!" Lefty said, nodding briskly.

"I know his name," Buttermaker said. "So?"

"He's trouble," said Lefty.

"Got a criminal mentality," said Engelberg.

"Been kicked out of four schools," said Regi.

"Even been BUSTED," Tanner said, "for MARIJUANA!"

"Done time for it in Juvenile Hall," said Ahmad.

"Oh?" said Buttermaker. "Who told you that?"

"HE did," Tanner said.

"In fact," said Ogilvie, taking a dramatic pause for inhaling asthma spray, "Kelly Leak is quite possibly the most dangerous twelve-year-old ever to walk the face of the earth."

"Well, Amanda should know something about . . ." Buttermaker turned. "Hey, Amanda?"

Amanda was already walking rapidly away toward the dugout. Buttermaker ran over and stopped her with a hand on her shoulder. "Hey, Amanda," he said softly, "what's the trouble? You know Kelly Leak. Why're you walking away?"

Amanda glanced back nervously at the Bears standing around the pitcher's mound. "You think I want all THEM to know Kelly's my boyfriend? They'd cut me dead. They all think Kelly's . . . crazy."

"You don't seem to think so, Amanda. What's the problem? Why isn't he playing?"

"He's had some, uh, difficulties here and there. The other teams won't touch him. And anyway, he thinks this is baby stuff."

"But look, everybody says he's a fantastic athlete. That ARM he's got! Hey, maybe if you talked to him—"

She spun on him. "Do your OWN recruiting, buster! I ain't talking to NOBODY! My deal is to pitch!"

"Okay, okay."

CHAPTER 6

The Bears were anxious with anticipation as they warmed up for their game with the Mets. Amanda stretched and flexed her arm, and several Bears stole glances often at their new prize. Engelberg tucked a big sponge into his catcher's mitt to absorb the sting of Amanda's pitches.

Buttermaker rapped out slow grounders to the infield, and many of them were fielded cleanly and thrown to first. In the outfield, Jimmy, Toby, and Ahmad looped tosses to one another.

Then Buttermaker walked Amanda to the mound, his arm around her shoulders. A buzz went through the stands at the vision of a girl taking the mound. There were a few hoots and jeers. Amanda looked straight ahead and ignored the taunts.

"Okay, Amanda," Buttermaker said, "take it easy in the beginning, loosen up slowly. You can let 'em hit a few, see how we handle it in the field."

She nodded. The umpire yelled, "PLAY BALL!"

"First batter for the Mets," came the announcement, "Bernie Sepcowiscz."

The Mets' leadoff hitter stepped up to the plate, accompanied by the cheers of his teammates on the bench.

Buttermaker stood in the dugout with one foot out on the grass. He leaned out and cupped his hands around his mouth to yell to his team: "Let's talk it up out there, Bears!"

Tanner spat into his glove and crouched down. "Come on, Mandy baby, fire it in there! No batter up there, nooo batter . . ."

"Rusty gate up there, no hitter," said Engelberg from behind the plate.

"Chuck it right past 'em, babe," called Ahmad from right.

"No troubles the batter," hollered Miguel from second, "we all behin' you . . ."

Buttermaker clamped his unlit Tiparillo between his teeth and clapped as Amanda went into her wind-up.

Her first pitch whacked into Engelberg's glove with Sepcowiscz never moving the bat from his shoulder.

"STEERIKE ONE!" the umpire called.

The Bears cheered. "Nooo batter up there . . ." " 'Nother one just like that, Mandy baby . . ." "Whooo, *tres tiros rapidos* . . ." "We on our way, Mandy!"

Ogilvie, standing in the dugout, gleefully punched his glove and belched some asthma medication. "Mandy's got her stuff today, Coach, I can FEEL it!"

Amanda eased up on the next pitch, and it was tapped slowly on the ground to short. Tanner wrenched his face in concentration, stooping low in a crouch, his left leg forward, his right leg behind his glove. The ball

118

bounced over his glove and hit his leg. He snatched it up and arced an accurate throw to Jose, who stretched forward, keeping one foot firmly on the bag, and took it for the out.

The Bears leaped and hollered; it was the first time they had ever put out the leadoff batter. Buttermaker thrust a fist into the air. "Way to dig it out, Tanner! Way to look that ball in, Jose!"

"Batting second," came the announcement, "and playing third today, CARL KARANSKY!"

Karansky, swinging three bats and obviously enjoying the high-pitched squeals of encouragement from girls in the stands, swaggered up to the plate.

Buttermaker, expecting Karansky to bat fourth, was caught momentarily by surprise. He jumped out of the dugout, yelling to the Bears: "THE COOL-CARL-KARANSKY SHIFT! THE SHIFT! HUSTLE IT UP!"

The Bears ran to their new positions, outfielders and infielders all to the left side, except Jose, who remained to cover first.

Karansky, confused, stepped out of the batter's box and looked down at his coach at third. The coach shrugged his shoulders.

"Come on, batter up!" said the umpire. "Don't hold up the game, Karansky."

Cool Carl stepped back in. Amanda threw an off-speed pitch, and Karansky slashed a low liner toward left. It bounced off Regi's glove, then off Miguel's shoulder, and popped up in the air behind the baseline. Ahmad waited stiffly under the ball, his glove in front of his face. Holding his breath, he made the catch.

The entire team raced up to hug him and slap his back. Ahmad tossed his cap into the air and flung the ball to Tanner, who threw it to Engelberg, who whipped it to Jose. It was relayed to every happy Bear; then Regi underhanded it back to Amanda.

Amanda took off her cap, swung her hair around, wiped off her forehead with her glove.

"Awright, Amanda," Buttermaker called, "let's go to work."

Amanda carefully adjusted her cap, wound up, and fired a smoker past the next batter. She followed that with two more, for her first strikeout, and the jubilant Bears came to bat.

It became a pitcher's duel. The innings slipped by quickly. Ahmad beat out a bunt in the third, for the Bears' only hit. The Mets got a Texas-league single in the fourth. The batter reached second on a passed ball by Engelberg, and third on a fielder's choice when Engelberg made a fine play on a topped roller in front of the plate and threw the batter out. Jose ended the threat when he knocked down a slow roller on the first-base line, picked it up, and tagged the runner going past.

In the last inning, with the score 0–0, Amanda eased off her fast ball, and the batter blooped it into right field, where Timmy Lupus had been substituted for Ahmad to play one inning. He ran toward it, but it hit just in front of him and bounced by. He hopped around crazily looking for it. He picked it up but, unsettled by the roar of the crowd, threw it not to the infield but to center.

Unfortunately, Toby Whitewood was no longer in center field. He had run over to help Timmy, and the ball rolled to the center-field fence.

Jimmy Feldman raced for it, lost his footing, and crashed into the fence. Dizzily he groped for the ball, and tossed it to Tanner. But the runner was already on his way to the plate, and Tanner's relay was too late.

The Bears came sadly off the field for their final time at bat, now trailing, 1–0.

Blood ran from Jimmy's nose, which was turning purple. "It's okay, Coach," he said, "it's—"

Buttermaker took Jimmy's face in his hands and looked closely at the nose. "It may be broken, Jimmy."

A doctor came down from the stands and took Jimmy away to his car.

The Bears, upset at letting the Mets score, and now worried about their injured teammate, struck out to end the game.

They sank into the dugout silently while the Mets gathered around home plate for the traditional cheer: "Two, four, six, eight—who do we appreciate? BEARS! BEARS! BEARS!"

Timmy Lupus, fighting back tears, took a seat at the far end of the dugout by himself.

Tanner paced back and forth, his teeth and fists clenched. "Lupus, you dumb spaz! We would have won if it weren't for you!"

"That's enough, Tanner," Buttermaker said.

"HECK, IF—"

"SHUT UP! He tried as hard as you did, as hard as anybody. We only got one hit, not enough to score a single run. You can't win with that. When we win, it'll be a team win. When we lose, it's a team loss."

The Bears all hung their heads. Buttermaker clapped his hands.

"Okay, snap out of it! Come on! The only important thing now is that we've got a game with the White Sox on Friday. And what does that mean?"

There was silence. Buttermaker slapped several shoulders. "WHAT DOES THAT MEAN?"

The Bears brought themselves together. They stood

up and raised their fists: BAD NEWS for the WHITE SOX!"

Buttermaker called the home of Jimmy Feldman and got no answer. Then he called Timmy Lupus. His mother answered.

"I know," she said in her soft voice, "I was there. I was proud that he played."

"I just hope that his one mistake didn't make him—"

"We got another call a little while ago," she said. "It was from Tanner Boyle. Timmy wouldn't come to the phone. But Tanner said that all he wanted was to tell Timmy to come out a little early tomorrow for some extra practice."

Buttermaker tried several more times to reach the Feldman home. Finally Mr. Feldman answered. "Yes, it's broken," he said. "Not too bad. Jimmy feels okay. But I guess you've lost another player."

Buttermaker muttered his apologies and regrets, then said, "Look, Mr. Feldman, please tell Jimmy we still want him out there, with the team. We can still use his eyes and ears and mouth and brain, even on the bench."

The Penny Arcade and Game Parlor was dimly lit, and populated by a seedy clientele that probably preferred it that way. Several men gathered around clanking, sparkling machines, loudly commenting on tiny tanks, rifle shots, and caroming steel balls.

A man in a torn work shirt and floppy hat stood at the end of a hockey table, opposing a boy in an angry game marked by curses and raps on the glass top. The boy was Kelly Leak.

The man slapped his fist against the side of the game and shook his head. He reached into his shirt pocket and pulled out a dollar bill and handed it to Kelly.

Kelly, an unlit cigarette dangling from his lips, quietly pocketed the money and called, "Next."

Buttermaker stepped up to the table. "I'm next."

Kelly looked up and froze. "What the devil are you—"

"I'm next," Buttermaker repeated, slipping a quarter into the slot. "I got the winner. You play a pretty mean game of table hockey, kid."

Kelly stood looking at him, making no move to play. "What are you doing here?"

"Playing hockey," Buttermaker said, "just like I said. I got the winner. Unless you own this place. Let's play."

The puck zipped around the table, propelled by sticks of spinning, sliding metal men. Both players hunched over the board, their hands on the levers that controlled the action.

"You come here often?" Buttermaker asked.

"Hunh?" Kelly looked up.

Buttermaker shot. "Goal," he said.

"Now wait a minute! You asked me a question . . ."

"Pay attention to the game," Buttermaker said, smiling impishly. "You're down a goal."

Kelly muttered a curse and bent over the game. The puck zoomed back and forth. Kelly rifled a shot, which Buttermaker skillfully parried. Buttermaker shot; Kelly stopped it.

"Saw you throw the ball from the parking lot the other day, kid," Buttermaker said, without interrupting his hockey moves. "You got a pretty fair arm." He maneuvered the puck toward Kelly's goal. "We could use a good outfielder."

Kelly got control of the puck and slammed in a goal. "You," he said scowling, "and a lot of other people."

Buttermaker smiled and started the puck moving again. "Maybe you'd like to play for us."

123

"For that bunch of BABIES? You gotta be . . ." Kelly looked up and Buttermaker slipped in a goal. "You sneaky—"

"I play to win," Buttermaker said softly, leaning forward over the table and grinning.

"Oh yeah?" Kelly bent down over the table with doubled intensity. "Well, who do you think can beat everybody in here?"

He fired two hard shots, which Buttermaker blocked and steered away. "What are we playing for, kid, sodas?"

"Sodas? SODAS!" Kelly blasted in a goal. "I don't drink sodas. Money, that's what we're playing for. Dollar a game."

"I don't play for money," Buttermaker said, starting the puck again.

"Beer, then. We'll play for beer."

"Beer?" He chortled. "Okay, beer. Watch yourself." He sent a screaming shot in for a goal. He looked up and smiled coolly. "How about a six-pack a game?"

"Fine. Let's go." Kelly sent several shots at Buttermaker's goal, but all were stopped. He grew angrier by the minute as frustration built in him. Several men gathered around and nodded gleefully at Buttermaker's quickness. "Why don't you losers BUTT OUT!" Kelly snapped. They laughed at him.

"For a guy who sees us as a bunch of babies," Buttermaker said, working the puck toward Kelly's end, "you sure hang around the field a lot."

"There's some neat broads down there," Kelly said, "that's why I hang around." He intercepted a pass and shot in the winning goal. "One six-pack," he snarled, "unless you wanna play some more."

"We'll play," Buttermaker said, his expression icy, "until you're tired."

Kelly scoffed. Buttermaker turned fierce, chewing savagely on his Tiparillo. His game became overpowering. He fired in shot after shot. Kelly gradually lost his composure, his nervous hands unable to control the men. The onlookers laughed and cheered and patted Buttermaker on the back as the score mounted.

Buttermaker won eight straight games, and finally Kelly slumped back against the wall, exhausted. His face was damp with sweat and red with humiliation. He closed his eyes. His cigarette dangled limply from his mouth.

Buttermaker flicked his lighter in Kelly's face, and Kelly jumped. Buttermaker put the flame to the end of Kelly's cigarette. "That's seven six-packs you owe me, kid, unless you wanna work 'em off."

"What do you mean by that?"

"Play for the Bears. A six-pack for every game you play."

"What a bunch a— Listen, dude! I ain't playin' in no kids' baseball team. One more game, double or nothing!"

Buttermaker tapped his watch. "I think it's getting a little late for growing boys."

"One more game! Unless you're scared!"

Buttermaker gazed at him. "I don't scare easily," he said.

"Neither do I! Come on!"

Buttermaker positioned himself behind the board and put in a quarter. He looked up at Kelly with a sly grin. "Too bad Amanda's not here to see this."

Kelly was completely disoriented. Buttermaker's first two shots went in.

"Fourteen six-packs, lad," Buttermaker said.

"It ain't fair," Kelly moaned, putting his head down on the glass and beating his fist on the side of the table. "I ain't even got that kind of money."

"Who said anything was fair?" Buttermaker said. He put his arm around Kelly's sagging shoulders and steered him toward the door. "By the way, Kelly Leak, can you hit?"

Tanner sat on a bench in the snack bar, munching on a hot dog. Near him stood Timmy Lupus, shifting uneasily from one foot to the other. His nose was running, and he sniffed loudly.

"Geez, Lupus, you crud!" said Tanner, wrinkling up his nose as he looked at his hot dog. "Could you go somewhere else while I'm tryin to EAT? You're makin' me sick!"

Timmy slunk away sadly, taking a seat on a distant bench.

Joey Turner and a Yankee teammate watched from the other side of the room. They nodded at each other, then moved over behind Timmy. Joey snatched Timmy's cap off his head and hid it behind his back.

Timmy jumped up. "Gimme it back," he said with a soft whine.

"Aw, what do you need it for?" Joey said. "You hardly ever play anyway."

"I want it," Timmy said.

Joey shook his head. Concealed from Timmy, Joey's teammate squirted ketchup into the hat.

"Gimme it," Timmy said, holding out his hand.

"Oh, okay, here."

Timmy took the cap and slapped it onto his head. Ketchup oozed down over his ears and forehead. He put a hand up to feel the slop, then looked at the mess on his fingers. His eyes became teary.

Joey and his friend giggled and then laughed.

Tanner sighed and got slowly up from his bench. He walked over to the two Yankees, both bigger than he.

"Hey, Joey," he said calmly, "you hungry? Here, you can have my hot dog. I can't eat any more."

"No thanks," Joey said, continuing to giggle at the sight of Timmy's head.

"Here, take it," Tanner said.

Joey shook his head. Tanner slammed the hot dog into Joey's face, then jammed his head into Joey's chest and began pounding his fists into his belly.

Joey flailed his arms to shove Tanner away. The other boy pinned Tanner's arms, and the two of them lifted Tanner up and flung him rear-first into a trash can. Joey gave him a solid shot on the top of the head, pounding him deeper into the can. The two Yankees guffawed and walked away.

Tanner, only his legs, arms, and head visible over the top of the can, spat at the floor.

Timmy came running over. He stopped just short of the can and looked shyly at his feet. "Nobody's ever . . . I mean . . . thanks for . . ."

"Hey, Lupus," Tanner said from his folded-up position, "if you wiped your nose once in a while, and stuck up for yourself more, and acted like a normal human being, people wouldn't give you crud all the time."

Timmy hung his head.

"Well, help me out of here," Tanner said, squirming to free himself, "we got a practice to get to."

Pigtails called Buttermaker into the equipment room. She stood with her hands on her hips, big legs spread apart, her hat pulled down just over her eyes.

"So, Buttermaker," she said, "you got that little Whurlizer girl pitching for you."

"Yeah. We were short, and we really can—"

"You musta figured I'd be calling you in here to crab about that."

"It crossed my mind, but since it's legal—"

"Listen, wiseacre, that's fine with me. I don't care what other people say, long as you take this league SE- RIOUS. That ain't why I called you in. It's THIS . . ."

She walked over and took his head in both hands and whispered into his ear.

He leaned back, surprised. "Really? I didn't know. Sorry. I'll take care of that first thing tomorrow."

"TODAY," Pigtails said.

"Today," Buttermaker agreed, nodding. He turned to leave.

"I declare," Pigtails chuckled, shaking her head, "I never thought I'D have to tell YOU about THAT."

"I get your point," Buttermaker said, smiling back.

He arrived at practice a few minutes late, gathered his team around, and began tossing out small orange boxes to them. "Something I forgot," he said. "Cups and supporters."

Several boys groaned.

"It's a league rule. They got to be worn at all times."

"Why do we have to wear them?" Toby asked, turn- ing his box slowly around in his hands to study the markings.

"That's a dumb question," Tanner said.

"They're awfully uncomfortable, you know," Engel- berg said.

"You either wear them or you don't play," Butter- maker said. "League rule."

"*Que es esto?*" Miguel said to Jose.

"*No se,*" Jose answered.

Jimmy Feldman, his nose heavily bandaged, leaned over to explain the new gear to the two boys.

They nodded, and then immediately began jabbering solemnly to each other in Spanish.

Buttermaker put his hands on his temples and closed

his eyes. "Will somebody please tell me what they're quacking about?"

Ogilvie inhaled some asthma medicine, then belched it out. He raised an index finger. "I've been brushing up on my Spanish of late," he said, "and I think they're saying something about being Catholic, and this might be some kind of sin or something."

"Oh, for heaven's sake, Jose and Miguel," Buttermaker said, "there's nothing in the—"

"Can we stop this already?" Tanner said, spitting on the grass. "We're late with practice."

"I don't like wearing this stuff, Coach Buttermaker," Engleberg said. "It's a free country. Let's take a democratic vote and see—"

"YOU AIN'T STRAPPING ONE OF THOSE THINGS ON ME!" Amanda suddenly erupted.

"Well, I guess in your case," Buttermaker said, "we might—"

"If she don't wear one, I don't wear one!" Engleberg said, pouting.

"Oh, for crying out loud, everybody!" Buttermaker sat down in the grass and closed his eyes.

"Hey, Coach!"

All eyes turned to see Kelly Leak strolling across the outfield grass, carrying a glove.

"I'm here to pay up," he said. "Let's get this show on the road. I ain't got all day."

Buttermaker scrambled to his feet and stuck out his hand, which Kelly ignored; then he turned, smiling, toward the open-mouthed team and said, "Boys, uh, Bears, you all know Kelly Leak. He's agreed to play in the outfield for us."

The Bears reacted with grunts and nods. Their chagrin at the presence of the notorious boy on their team was balanced by their obvious awe at his athletic talents.

Amanda stood with her head down. Kelly walked up to her, looked her over cockily, and said, "So this is your new pitcher, hunh? Well, come on, pitcher, let's see what you got."

Kelly picked up a bat and headed for the plate, while Amanda walked to the mound.

"One thing she ain't got is one of THESE," Engelberg grumbled, tossing his orange box into the dugout.

"Shut up, Engleberg," Tanner said. "This is embarrassing ENOUGH!"

"Yeah, well, you got a hot-dog paper stuck to your tail, Tanner!"

Tanner quickly brushed it off.

Amanda wound up and threw a medium-speed ball to Kelly. He caught it in his bare hand and smiled confidently. "Little harder, hunh?"

"This turkey thinks he's Mickey Mantle," Amanda mumbled to the surrounding Bears. She gathered herself and spun a sharp-breaking curve.

Kelly had anticipated it, and let it go by. "Come on," he called, "ain't you got no fast ball?"

Amanda did a double windup and cut loose with a hummer, right across the letters. Kelly swung and connected. All eyes followed the ball as it soared over the left-field fence.

Kelly tossed down his bat and picked up his glove. "Let's practice," he said.

The White Sox were fifth in the standings, just two from the bottom, which meant that they were a formidable opponent for the lowly Bears. But the Bears, with their two new acquisitions, were hopeful of getting their first win, or coming close.

The stands were about half full—would probably be full for the second game, which pitted the unbeaten Yankees against the second-place Mets.

The first three Bears struck out, as did the first three White Sox. Leading off the second inning was Kelly Leak. He took two strikes without moving his bat, then calmly stroked the third pitch high over the center-field fence for a homer.

Bedlam surrounded him, and a dozen hands reached out to slap his back as he arrived at the Bears' dugout.

Immediately the White Sox manager trotted over to where Pigtails was sitting in the stands. "Since when is that little hoodlum playing?" he asked angrily.

"I ain't necessarily a fan of his any more than you are," she said, "but his birth certificate says he's twelve, and that's the only requirement."

"All right, then." He stuck a finger in her face. "I'm playing this game under protest. Rules say that every manager has to be notified of a new player ahead of time."

"Aw, so what's new?" Pigtails said, waving him away. "You play every game under protest. Get back out there and coach."

"Come on," the umpire called, "PLAY BALL!"

Kelly's one run was all the Bears needed. Amanda threw nothing but goose-eggs, striking out eight—mixing in a few curves just to keep her touch. She allowed only one solidly hit ball, a low liner to left, which Kelly saved with a diving catch.

With the final out, all the Bears converged on Amanda, yelling and hugging her, and waving their index fingers in the air—not because they were number one, but because they had won for their first time.

Roy Turner bounced down from the stands and ran over to Buttermaker, grabbing his elbow. "Hey, Buttermaker, what the devil is this? First you got a girl playing, then a crook. What are you trying to do to us?"

"Beat you," Buttermaker said, swinging his arm away, "that's all."

"When THAT day comes," Turner called after him as he walked away, "my boys will want to hang up their gloves forever. Meanwhile . . ."

Buttermaker turned back toward him. "Yeah?"

"You just . . . watch your step."

Outside the snack bar, Councilman Whitewood tapped Buttermaker on the shoulder. "Hey, chum," he said with quiet seriousness, "I'm not sure I like the looks of things, what's going on."

"What's the trouble, Bob? We won a ball game, didn't we?"

"Yeah, sure. But to have that little girl playing, and now that PUNK. You know, we have to be concerned with how the league LOOKS, I mean, to other people who might—"

"Bob, I don't give a hang about how the league looks. I'm coaching the Bears. We're gonna win some ball games now, and we're gonna look GOOD."

"Try to understand me, old pal. Winning and losing isn't that important—either way, I don't care. It's just that I'm not sure I want to be associated with—"

"Then don't be associated with it, friend." Buttermaker reached into his pocket and pulled out Whitewood's latest check. He casually tore it to shreads and held the pile out to Whitewood. "A good suggestion on what to do with this would be to stuff it in your ear. Excuse me, please. I'm gonna join my team in the snack bar."

Buttermaker preferred to have things pleasant, to allow people to go their own way so long as they allowed him to go his. But he was not afraid to stand his ground, to tell people off when it was warranted. However, since he was generally mild-mannered and quiet, people toward whom he directed his occasional outbursts were liable to be shocked. He knew his old friend Whitewood had been shocked. But that was all right. Whitewood had a lot of things going on in his life. Besides, Whitewood knew him well enough to be aware that Buttermaker could not be pushed around forever.

Roy Turner was another matter. Turner disturbed him. There was something in the man's nastiness, his intensity, that suggested to Buttermaker that he might welcome—even need—friendship. Buttermaker did not ordinarily reach out for people, not lately at least. But he felt it was time to change, to come out of his shell. So he decided to make Turner his friend, or at least not his enemy.

He approached the Turners' front door, which was not brightened by the floodlight so common to front yards in this well-to-do neighborhood. Turner was a Pontiac dealer, and apparently a successful one.

Buttermaker squinted to locate the buzzer in the darkness. He was about to press it when he heard voices inside, angry voices.

"You might as well know," Jill Turner said in a biting voice, "that I don't care so much as a TOENAIL about your damn championship team! It's all so CHILDISH! Why can't you live like a blasted ADULT?"

Roy Turner sat staring at the carpet. "I work as hard as anybody," he said sullenly.

"Selling CARS, as if THAT was a big deal."

"It gives you everything you want."

She cackled meanly. "Everything I want? You must be kidding. You mean the house? The pool? Spending money? What I want is somebody around here I can talk to, enjoy being with, respect—not a darn baseball pipsqueak."

He looked up at her. "You never DID think it was important, did you, helping out a bunch of kids?"

"You're not helping them out. You just yell and scream and make them afraid of you. Just so they'll win their damned championships."

"It's important."

"To YOU it's important. More than to the kids. And it's certainly not important to me."

"What about Joey?"

"I'd rather he grew up thinking other things were more important than winning baseball games."

"What's important to you?"

"Have MERCY! After all these years, you still don't know. Life is important, adults. Having fun. Being with a man."

"I'm man enough."

She scoffed. "Who knows? Being a man isn't just running around flexing your muscles. You don't talk. Except about the damned Yankees. Who knows what's going on in your mind?"

"Do you want to know?"

"No. For heaven's sake, no. I'm afraid I would be disappointed."

"You didn't used to be. I haven't changed. I'm still the same Roy Turner you used to like to talk to."

"Well, SOMETHING'S changed. Maybe I'VE changed. I'm bored. You don't know me anymore."

"I wish I did."

"Crap."

"I do."

"Double crap. You don't care about anything except the blessed Yankees . . ."

Buttermaker slowly sucked the flame in to the end of his cigar and blew a steady stream of smoke into the night air. Then he walked down the steps and back to his car.

The third-place Cubs were tough. They scored two quick runs on two infield hits and four errors. Then Amanda started giving them curve balls.

In the field, the Bears worked hard. A pop fly brought Ahmad hustling in. He held his glove high, stumbled, caught the ball, and did three somersaults. Then he scrambled to his feet and held the ball aloft triumphantly, bringing cheers from the Bears and the stands.

A hard liner bounced off Regi's chest at third. With shock still registered on his face, Regi picked it up and threw the runner out.

Finally, in the sixth, the Bears loaded the bases: Tanner beat out a grounder, Engleberg walked, and Jose reached on an error. That brought up Kelly Leak, who had gone down once on a called third strike—which he disputed—and twice on good catches in the outfield.

This time he lined the first pitch smashing into the left-field fence. Tanner crossed the plate. Engelberg lumbered around third. Jose, much faster, was right on his heels.

"Andale, andale, Engelberk!" he shouted. *"Ap-uarte!"*

Engelberg huffed and puffed toward home. The ball was relayed to the shortstop, who whirled and threw to the catcher. The catcher took the throw and faced the oncoming Engelberg.

Engelberg lowered his head and blasted into the catcher, who went catapulting backward and dropped the ball. Engelberg landed flat on his face across home plate, his rotund body completely covering it.

The catcher sat up and shook his head dizzily. Jose danced around Engelberg frantically, trying to find a bit of the plate to touch.

"GET OFF THE PLATE, YOU BLIMP!" Tanner screamed. "LET JOSE SCORE!"

But Engelberg was stunned, and was barely moving.

The catcher retrieved the ball and began chasing Jose around Engelberg's prone form.

Finally, like a beached and dying whale, Engelberg rolled over, and Jose dove for the plate, just under the catcher's lunging tag.

"SAFE!" shouted the umpire. "BOTH SAFE!"

The Bears' dugout erupted in cheers as the Bears came rushing out. They had beaten the Cubs, 3-2, for their second win.

The Bears sat together at McDonald's, eating hamburgers and french fries and slurping sodas. Ahmad proudly displayed the rip in his uniform suffered in his acrobatic catch in right.

Timmy Lupus turned his head away to blow his nose privately.

Engelberg rubbed the bruises where Jose had kicked him trying to get a foot on the plate.

Amanda massaged her right elbow, which had stiffened up slightly.

Jimmy Feldman winced every time an arm came near his bandaged nose, and Lefty Stein reacted similarly in protecting his wrist.

"Where you going, Kelly?" Buttermaker said.

"Aw, I ain't much for sodas," Kelly said, disappearing out the door.

"I have the scouting report on the Athletics," Ogilvie said to Buttermaker, plopping a stack of notes on the table and adjusting his glasses for reading.

"Tomorrow," Buttermaker said in weary happiness. He slapped Oglivie on the knee. "We'll go over them tomorrow. Tonight we relax. Our season is just beginning."

Indeed, the Bears were rolling. They won their next game from the Athletics, 3-1. Timmy Lupus allowed the Mets to score, giving them a 1-0 lead, when he dropped a ball in right, picked it up, and threw it about eight feet, ran after it and threw again, ten feet, then finally fell down and handed it to Miguel, who threw to the plate too late.

The Bears got their win by virtue of a two-run homer by Kelly in the fourth and his triple in the sixth, followed by his steal of home.

Now they were to face the White Sox again. Having beaten them once, the Bears were anxious to play.

Buttermaker, Pigtails, and the White Sox met at home plate prior to their scheduled game. The White Sox coach shook his head morosely.

"Three of my players got the flu," he said. "Another one, his parents took him off to some revival meeting in Bakersfield. Another one, his father said he was falling behind in school and he won't let him play. I only got eight boys here today."

"Well, the rules say you'll have to forfeit the game," Pigtails said, putting a hand gently on his shoulder. "And that's the way it has to be."

"Sorry," the coach said.

"So are we," Buttermaker said. "We don't like to win this way."

Buttermaker went back to his team and made the announcement. At first the Bears were disappointed; they had looked forward to the game.

"Hey!" Ogilvie said. "That means we're .500 for the season!"

At that, the Bears brightened dramatically.

"We're FOUR AND FOUR!" Tanner yelled, jumping up and down.

"EVEN UP!" Ahmad hollered, hugging Tanner and dancing around in a circle. "Imagine THAT!"

The joyful Bears gathered for the cheer: "Two, four, six, eight—who do we appreciate? WHITE SOX! WHITE SOX! WHITE SOX! YEEAA!"

They tossed their caps into the air and danced and cheered until their legs collapsed and they were gasping for breath. Then they headed for their bicycles.

Next up were the Mets, who had been holding down second place, behind the Yankees. Amanda tired in the late innings, having mixed in a bunch of curve balls, and gave up a two-run homer to Carl Karansky. But Kelly got two triples to drive in three runs, and the Bears won, 4-2.

They were above .500, and rising.

Then Amanda put down the White Sox (their full team intact), 5-0, on just one hit, while striking out eleven. Kelly homered, Engelberg doubled to right center, Tanner bounced a triple off the left-field fence, and Ahmad beat out two bunts.

And behind Amanda's tiring arm, they won a slugfest from the Indians, 10-8, Kelly getting three homers and Tanner one.

Attitudes toward and within the Bears changed.

CHAPTER 7

"I don't see how ANYBODY'S gonna beat us," said Jimmy Feldman, pacing back and forth across the living room and fingering the bandage on his nose. "We're SENSATIONAL. I just wish I could play."

"In a week, maybe," his father said.

"Wow, we're just eating people UP, Dad."

"Well, you've won a few, all right."

"I mean, like those WHITE SOX, for example. They're RIDICULOUS. Whether they got enough play-ers or not, we just walk all over them. We just LAUGH at 'em."

"Take it easy, now, Jimmy, take it easy . . ."

Mike Engelberg took six bites of his supper, then shoved his chair back and stood up.

"Mikey, what?" his mother asked.

"Gotta do some running, Ma. Gonna run around the block."

"What is this running, Michael?" his father asked.

"We didn't do laps today at practice. Coach is gettin' soft."

"You can't run without nourishment, Mikey," his mother said, looking at him sadly.

"Maybe I'll eat later, Ma, after I run. Don't wanna be like the Yankees, they're all fatties. Know what I been hearing? I been hearing that I'm the fastest catcher in the league."

Ahmad tossed a tennis ball against the steps and caught the popped-up rebounds in various unorthodox positions—behind his back, between his legs, sometimes with eyes closed.

"What's this stuff?" his brother asked, coming out of the house. "You some kind of sideshow player? And shouldn't you be using two hands to catch?"

"Two hands is for beginners," Ahmad said. "I already got that DOWN. I'm workin on the harder stuff."

"Hmm," his brother said, "ordinary fly balls ain't hard enough for you, hunh?"

"Shoot," Ahmad said, dropping one he tried to backhand, "the way WE goin', there ain't hardly no business for me at ALL out there in right."

"What's wrong with a girl pitching, Dad?" Toby Whitewood asked.

"It's not that I have anything girls playing baseball," Councilman Whitewood said. "It's just that I think girls would be happier playing with other girls."

"But there isn't any TEAM for girls, and Coach Buttermaker said—"

His father slammed down his magazine. "I'm TIRED of hearing about Coach Buttermaker! It's Coach Buttermaker did this, Coach Buttermaker said that. It's you BOYS that have to play the games, you and your famous GIRL PITCHER."

"But we're winning with her pitching. Isn't that important, after what we went through in the beginning?"

"Winning isn't the most important thing. Looking like a decent team is. And now you've got that juvenile delinquent, Kelly Leak. A girl pitching, and Kelly Leak too."

"Yeah, but those two that you don't like are our best players, and they practice just as hard as any—"

"Will you please leave me alone and let me read?"

"Sorry. I got a hit yesterday."

"Mmm."

Lefty Stein unwrapped the Ace bandage and flexed his wrist. The swelling was gone, and most of the soreness, but it felt stiff and weak. He wound up in a pitching motion, and winced.

His little sister leaned against the kitchen door, rattling some jacks in her hand. "What are you doing THAT for, stork-bones, you aren't gonna pitch anymore."

"Who says, diaper-pail?"

"A girl's better than you," she tittered.

Lefty hurled his glove at her as she disappeared down the hall.

"Let's see YOU make this team, barf-breath!" he hollered after her, rubbing his wrist, which throbbed from the throw. "You couldn't even sit on the BENCH!"

"I just want you to know," said Regi Tower's father, "that we're very proud of you."

"I haven't done much," Regi said. "Mandy and Kelly are doing it all."

"That's what I mean," his father said, scowling. "It takes GUTS just to STOMACH those two misfits on your team."

"Hey!" Reggie flared.

"Now, now, Regi and Papa," his mother said, "let's be nice . . ."

"Who do you think stopped that LINER yesterday," Regi said angrily, "with his CHEST? Wasn't that—"

"Try and use your glove next time, boy."

"Winning, winning, winning," said Mr. Agilar, shaking his head, "that's all you two talk about."

"That's all we DO now," said Jose.

"Every game," said Miguel.

"You're lucky to have those two stars on your team," Mr. Agilar said.

"When we win . . ." said Jose.

"It's a team win," said Miguel.

"And when you lose?" their father said, leaning forward toward them.

"We DON'T lose," Miguel said.

"Not with THOSE two playing," Jose said.

"It's exciting, isn't it," Mrs. Lupus said, "winning all those games?"

"Especially when you got a friend like Tanner on the team," Timmy said.

She raised her eyebrows. "Tanner Boyle? I thought he was the one that yelled at you all the time."

"He's the one that TALKS to me," Timmy said happily.

"You can clearly see," said Ogilvie, "that my point is being borne out."

"It might be argued," his father said, polishing his

thick glasses, "that it isn't so much the law of averages that is being substantiated, but the historical element of the heroic ingredient. With the addition of those two stellar players, the team is basically transformed, not the same one about which you stated your theory."

"All that is taken into account," Ogilvie said. "Something GOOD was bound to happen to the Bears."

"And now"—his father smiled—"something BAD?"

Ogilvie was taken aback. "Something bad?"

"Your law of averages, my son, must continue to operate."

"Oh no, no, no, no," said Ogilvie, briskly shaking his head. "A natural balance has now been reached. We shall win the championship."

Tanner sat rapt before the television.

"Tanner," his sister said, "I'd like to—"

"Leave me alone. I'm watching my favorite show."

"—talk to you about your friend, Kelly Leak."

"Hunh?" He turned to her.

"How old's he, fifteen?"

"Who cares?"

"My friend Gloria would like to meet him. Maybe you could—"

"Buzz off! MOM would probably like to meet him."

"What a nasty thing to—"

"Come ON! This is my favorite show!"

"HEY!" yelled Kelly above the screaming of his parents. "CAN'T you two stop fighting? PLEASE?"

His father spun and shoved him violently against the wall. "SHUT UP, YOU LOUD-MOUTHED PUNK! YOU AIN'T BIG ENOUGH YET TO TALK TO ME!"

"Please, Hank," Kelly's mother said, "leave the kid alone."

"As for YOU, woman!" His father pushed her against another wall. "I so much as SEE you talkin' to another guy, I'll whip you PURPLE!"

Kelly started to run out of the room. His father stopped him and spun him around. "And as for you, kid," he hissed savagely. "You stay away from that little wench, and stay away from that baseball field, or no-body'll recognize that face of yours when I get through with it! You're trouble for me everywhere you go!"

"He's a good coach, that's all I know," Amanda said, nibbling at her supper.

"He never mentions, I mean, what does he talk about?" Brenda asked.

"He never talks about nothing, sis."

"Anything, Amanda."

"Anything."

"Aren't you afraid that you might, uh, hurt yourself, playing baseball?"

"Of course not. Hey, sis, you gotta stop worrying about me. I can take care of myself. You worry too much about everybody. People can handle their own af-fairs."

"Amanda, you're only eleven, and—"

"And I'm playing baseball with people my age. Aren't you glad we're WINNING, by the way?"

"Are you?"

"Come on, you know we are. Don't give me that. I see you reading the sports page."

Brenda chuckled. "I shouldn't try to fool you."

"You CAN'T," Amanda said, smiling at her.

Next up was the Cubs. The Bears, having already beaten them once, 3-2, looked forward to trouncing them this time.

All the Bears except Kelly and Amanda arrived at the field early and commenced happy, carefree horsing around, combined with a little warming up. From time to time heads turned toward the parking lot for signs of their two stars.

Game time approached. Finally Amanda appeared, walking slowly through the parking lot, wearing a sweatshirt with the hood tightly tied around her face.

She walked into the dugout and sat down, and sneezed. All the Bears came running over to greet her, then stood still and stared. She was pale and sweaty, and sneezed often. Ogilvie handed her a Kleenex.

"Id's all ride, Coach," she said, sniffing. "I'll be okay in a few minudds."

"It's NOT all right, Amanda," Buttermaker said, feeling her brow. "You're really sick. You shouldn't even be here."

"Well, I AMB, and I ain'd leaving."

"You ain't playing, either. Where's Kelly?"

"Haven'd the faindest idea. How would I know?" She sneezed and wiped her nose. She hung her mouth open, closed her eyes, and pulled the sweatshirt tight around her.

"Holy mackerel, Coach!" Tanner said. "What're we gonna do?"

"What do you mean, what are we gonna do?"

"Well, geez." He hooked a thumb at Amanda. "She can't play, and Kelly ain't here . . ."

"So, we'll do with what we have. This team isn't just two players."

"Practically," Engelberg said.

"In fact," said Ogilvie, "I think the statistics would

show that Mandy and Kelly between them are responsible for—"

"Knock it off, crybabies!" Buttermaker said. "Take the field, Bears. Ogilvie, you go to left. Lupus, right. Ahmad, you play center. And, Whitewood . . ."

Toby, afraid he was dropped from the lineup, was standing wide-eyed at the rear of the group.

". . . You pitch."

"Pitch?"

"Right. Let's go, everybody warm up."

"Geez!" said Engelberg. "Whitewood pitching!"

"And you better not drop one, Engelberg," Buttermaker said.

The Bears took the field.

"Tell me, Amanda," Buttermaker said, "where in blazes is Kelly?"

"I TOLD you, I haven'd the faindest idea. I'm nod his mother. He lives his life, I live mide."

Lefty Stein walked over. "I think I could play, Coach, if—"

"Save that wrist, Lefty. If you can play at all, we'll need you at the end of the season."

"Doc says I'll have the bandage off my nose in a couple of days," Jimmy Feldman said.

"Good, good. But for now, you guys take it easy."

They walked off to watch warm-up, leaving Buttermaker and Amanda alone.

"Amanda, where is he?"

"We had a fight. I think he quit. He went off to fide some muddy somewhere, he said it was to buy you some beer. Whad's thad all aboud?"

"Oh, just something between us. You really think he quit?"

"Who knows? Nobody knows everything aboud Kelly Leak."

"Mmm."

"I'm sorry I god sick."

He tapped her head gently and smiled, realizing suddenly how young she was, how small, how close. Yet how grown-up and distant at the same time. Kids were not to figure out, any more than adults. People were mysterious. Buttermaker sighed. "Well, I got a game to coach."

He walked out to the diamond. Roy Turner walked by, heading for the stands. Turner stopped and scanned the field. "Hey, Buttermaker," he called, loud enough for the entire stands to hear, "your team looks more normal today. Glad you came around, if you know what I mean!"

Buttermaker hunched his shoulders against Turner's voice. "Okay, Bears, let's go. Get the first batter. On your toes."

The Bears gave up three runs in the first, on two walks, a double, and two errors. Toby Whitewood also struck out two batters, mainly because they were overanxious to swing at his blooper pitches.

Between innings, Tanner sat next to Amanda. "Sorry you're sick," he said.

"Nobody's sorrier than I amb," she said, peering out from the slit she had left in the sweatshirt hood for her eyes.

"I'll get a hit for you," he said as his time came to bat.

"Fide," Amanda said.

Tanner delivered a single, a grounder past the pitcher into center, and smiled proudly in from first to Amanda, in the dugout.

But the Cubs had little difficulty with Toby Whitewood, blasting him for seven more runs, and twice sending him pancaking on his belly to escape screaming liners up the middle. The Bears managed three runs, thanks to a dozen walks served up by the Cubs' pitcher.

The 10–3 loss dropped the Bears' record to seven wins and five losses. They next faced the awesome, still-undefeated Yankees, who had beaten them 21–0 in the season opener. And Amanda seemed a doubtful starter for the game.

That night, Buttermaker cruised the downtown streets, looking for Kelly Leak's motorcycle. He asked at the Penny Arcade, and was told that Kelly hadn't been there in a couple of days. He checked the various cyclists' haunts, but saw no small black Harley.

Finally he pulled into the dark North Valley League parking lot to think. On the one hand, Buttermaker thought that it was ridiculous for an eleven-year-old girl and a twelve-year-old boy to be going together and then to have a fight and behave just like adults.

On the other hand, there he was, an adult, acting just like a child by worrying about winning baseball games. But there was no question about it: He was infected just like the Bears with the delights of winning.

He sure wished he could find Kelly Leak and talk him out of this silly business of quitting just because he had a fight with his girlfriend. He sure wished he could find him, mainly because he really needed him against the Yankees.

Ridiculous! Childish! Here he wanted to find Kelly Leak because he needed him, while Kelly Leak didn't need Buttermaker at all. "What a topsy-turvy business," he muttered to himself. Kids were supposed to need ADULTS, not the other way around.

What a lousy break, he thought, to lose his two key players.

But then, he admitted, he had got two good breaks in

finding them when the Bears were losing—why shouldn't it balance out with two bad breaks when they were winning?

Besides, he was forced further to admit, he kept coming back to the fact that what was bothering him most was not Kelly's welfare, or Amanda's, but the prospect of losing baseball games. In a way, it was Kelly who was the mature one, because he didn't care about winning games, and it was Buttermaker who was immature, because he did.

"Oh, knock it off, Buttermaker," he muttered aloud, chuckling. "Quit thinking the thing to death, and relax. Nobody else cares as much about all this as you do, so just relax."

He was pondering the moon and the vacant baseball field below it when another car slowly pulled in beside his. Its lights went off.

A figure got out and came over to his open window. "Hi," said Jill Turner, "thought I'd find you here."

"Hello," he said. "Why'd you think that?"

She giggled. "Oh, I heard you came here to . . . relax."

Buttermaker recalled briefly with embarrassment his earlier nighttime bouts with the bottle in this parking lot. "Sometimes," he said.

"May I get in?"

"Uh, sure."

She walked around and got in, sliding over close to him. "What are you thinking about, Morris?"

"Nothing much. Baseball."

She put her hand on his arm. "Can't anybody around here think of anything but baseball?"

"Such as?"

"Oh, me, for instance."

"What should I think about you?"

"Well, you could think about what kind of life I have."

"What kind is that?"

"Try to imagine what it's like, living with somebody who—"

"Hey, Jill," Buttermaker interrupted, "everybody's got problems to work out with somebody. As a matter of fact, I was just thinking about Kelly Leak. You see, it's a kind of interesting situation, because I'm looking for Kelly, who's missing because he had a fight with—"

Jill suddenly threw her arms around him. "Please, Morris, I'm so—"

"Hold it," he said, gently removing her arms from around his neck and pushing her away. "Look, Jill, I like you. And I'm not dumb. If you've got a problem with Roy, you have to work that out with him, not with me. I may seem conveniently available, but I'm not really. I have my own problems to work out, with . . . somebody."

She sat back in a pout. "Sorry. I didn't know you had somebody."

"That's not the point, whether I've got somebody or not. The point is, you work out your problems where they exist. You don't run away from them."

Buttermaker turned away, embarrassed by his own hypocrisy. Nobody ran away from problems more than he. He felt that his words were correct, but that he had no business saying them.

"I thought," Jill said softly, "that maybe I was attractive to you."

"You ARE, of course you are. Nobody could deny that you're a very attractive woman. I'm just saying that I'm not a solution to your problems, any more than you're a solution to mine."

"What are your problems, Morris?"

"Same as everybody's, nothing special."

She looked away from him, out the window. "What did you mean about working out my problems with Roy?"

He thought for a moment. "I don't know. You might consider whether or not HE'S happy."

"Why SHOULDN'T he be? He's got everything he wants, his marvelous Yankees."

"And you? Has he got you?"

She blushed and hung her head.

"I don't know," Buttermaker said. "He doesn't seem happy to me. He seems angry. You guys should talk more, about what's really on your minds. Something like that." He grew increasingly uneasy. "I can't advise anybody."

They sat for a few minutes in silence.

"I didn't mean to embarrass you," she said at last.

"You didn't."

She pushed open the car door. "Thank you for talking to me."

"Talk is cheap."

She got into her car and drove out of the lot.

"Whew!" Buttermaker said aloud.

The Yankees had already won twelve straight, and sewed up first place. Their star, coach's son Joey Turner, was batting .759, and had pitched four no-hitters, leading the league in both departments.

The Bears were depressed. Amanda was still recovering from the flu.

The Yankees were clearly overconfident. They warmed up lackadaisically, joking, laughing, throwing balls behind their backs and between their legs.

The Bears looked on with rising anger. Finally Engelberg stalked out to the edge of the infield and yelled at Joey Turner: "You got BAD NEWS coming, you jerk pitcher!"

"Oh yeah?" Turner called back, grinning meanly.

"YEAH!" Tanner shouted from the dugout.

"Okay, boys," Buttermaker said, "knock it off. We got a game to play."

Toby walked the first two batters, got the third on a called strike, then watched with dismay as a ball off the bat of Joey Turner soared over the left-field fence for a home run.

Turner swaggered around the bases, and thumbed his nose at Engelberg as he crossed the plate.

Already down 3–0 when they came to bat, the Bears were filled with frustration and anger. Regi Tower and Ahmad struck out quickly. Engelberg stepped in and glared out at Joey.

Joey smiled back devilishly. He wound up and threw. Engelberg flopped to the ground as the pitch just missed his head. The umpire waved a cautionary finger at Joey. The second pitch came even closer.

Now the umpire took off his mask and called Roy Turner out of the dugout. Buttermaker also came trotting over. "I believe your pitcher is throwing at the batter deliberately, Mr. Turner," the umpire said. "I don't want to have to throw him out of the game."

Turner stood staring at the umpire, his face growing red with embarrassment as he felt Buttermaker's eyes on him.

"What are you gonna do about it, Turner," Buttermaker asked sternly.

Turner clenched and unclenched his fists as he stood, mortified and uncertain. Suddenly he whirled and ran out to the mound. "You throw at that guy?" he barked at Joey. "YOU THROW AT THAT GUY?" Joey hung his head. His father swung his right hand and smacked

Joey across the face with his open palm. Joey's knees buckled. Then he straightened up and stared, wet-eyed, straight into his father's face.

Roy Turner cursed and strode away from the mound. He crossed the third-base line and suddenly stood face-to-face with Jill, who had run down from the stands. They stared at each other silently.

Then, abruptly, Jill turned on her heel and walked off the field.

"Play ball," the umpire said.

Joey tossed a soft pitch to Engelberg, who slapped a high-bouncer back to the mound. Joey caught it, then stood motionless as Engelberg rumbled down to first.

Roy Turner sprang to the edge of the dugout and looked out, shocked and confused, saying nothing.

Joey folded his arms. Buttermaker sensed the situation instantly. "SECOND, ENGELBERG, GO TO SECOND!"

Engelberg started, stopped, danced around, not knowing what to do. He started walking hesitantly toward second, an eye on Joey. Joey, still holding the ball, turned away from him, his arms still folded.

Engelberg picked up speed, slipped, fell, rolled over, got up, and fell onto second base. He looked around quickly at Joey, who still had his back to him.

"THIRD, ENGELBERG, THIRD!"

Engelberg, now giggling uncontrollably, skipped merrily down to third base.

The Yankees converged on Joey, yelling and screeching, and tried to wrestle the ball away. Joey swung and kicked to beat them off. The whole bunch of them, Joey in the middle, fell to the ground in a squirming, yowling knot.

"HOME, ENGELBERG, HOME!"

Engelberg, now frightened by the screaming, struggling mass of league-leading Yankees a few feet away from him, set off in a mad dash for the plate, his eyes wide with terror. Twenty feet from home, he began his slide. Ten feet from home, he slid to a stop. He got to his knees and crawled frantically the rest of the way in a cloud of dust, finally sitting on home plate, gasping for breath, his face a mask of grime and sweat.

Instantly, Joey gave up the ball to his teammates, who then stood around him silently, gazing into their dugout.

Roy Turner stood with his head down.

The Bears cheered, but in a subdued manner, almost ashamed, and gathered around Engelberg to brush him off.

"Play ball," the umpire said.

The game returned at once to normal, almost as if nothing had happened. Normal meaning that the Yankees, taking advantage of Toby's weak arm and the Bears' collision-course fielding that left Regi, Tanner, Ahmad, and Miguel bruised and dazed, blasted balls all over the field and poured runs across the plate.

Even Joey returned to normal, striking out ten Bears, and belting a homer and a double and two singles.

The Yankees won, 12–2.

The Bears drifted silently away from the field. Tanner caught up with Amanda in the parking lot.

"Hey, Mandy, hey!"

"Hey, Tanner."

"Tough game," he said, falling in beside her. "Too bad you weren't playing. We would have won."

"Maybe."

"And Kelly too, we needed him."

"Mmm."

"How you feeling, Mandy?"

"Better."

"Good, that's really good." Tanner looked around casually. "I was wondering," he said, turning his head this way and that to look at everything but Amanda, "if, uh, maybe you'd like to join me in a Coke or something. That is, of course, if you're feeling good enough."

"No, I . . ." Amanda stopped and looked at Tanner thoughtfully. "Oh, what the heck. Sure I will. Come on." She looped her arm through his, and they walked off together.

Down the block, concealed between two parked cars, Kelly Leak sat aboard his Harley. He watched the two ambling away arm-in-arm. He grabbed his two rearview mirrors and violently wrenched them off.

Despite their two short-handed losses, the Bears were still alive—barely—in the race for second place. The Mets, currently in second, had just one game left, and would almost certainly win that, for it was against the poor, last-place White Sox, who had won just one game, the early one against the Bears, and who were getting weaker every week.

The Bears were tied for third with the Indians, in a half game behind the Mets. If the Bears beat both the Indians, in their next game, and then the Athletics, in their final one, they would end in a second-place tie with the Mets.

The frustrating thing about that was that, in the event of a tie for second, the determination of which team would play the Yankees for the championship would be made on the basis of which team had the best runs-for-and-against record.

The Bears, alas, by virture of their atrocious start and their last two debacles, had scored nine runs fewer than the Mets, and had allowed twenty-two more against them. So if there was a tie, the Mets would be in the championship.

But Buttermaker had urged them on, convincing them that to achieve a tie for second in their first season would be an amazing success, "worthy," as he put it, "of banner headlines, if the sports editors had any brains."

So they would fight for the tie.

Ogilvie and Engelberg sat on the ground under a big evergreen tree in the woods that bordered the freeway. "You sure we should be doing this?" asked Engelberg nervously.

"I cannot honestly say that I'm sure we SHOULD be doing it," Ogilvie answered, "but it is my conviction that if we are to beat the Indians, we MUST do it."

"Geez, I don't know . . ."

"Look, Engelberg, I'M the one taking the risk. You don't even have to BE here if you don't want. It's just that I consider ourselves the Bears' scouting team, and this is part of scouting, in a way."

"What if the guy don't show?"

"He will, believe me."

"Look, Ogilvie." Engelberg started to get up. "Maybe this isn't necessary at all. Mandy may be able to pitch, then our problems are—"

"And who's going to hit, may I ask you? If they score a single run against us, we are finished. No, my friend, this is absolutely essential. We are engaged in the most crucial service to our team. Anyway, we're DOING it."

Engelberg sat back down, fidgeting with leaves and looking around nervously.

There was a rustle a distance away, and a small figure appeared, nearing them under the boughs.

"Here's our Indian," Ogilvie whispered, elbowing Ogilvie in the ribs.

The boy came up to them and sat down. They all nodded silent greetings. The Indian player wore several gaudy rings and beaded necklaces. One shirt pocket bulged with a pack of cigarettes, the other with a deck of cards. His cowboy boots were brightly polished, his porkpie hat was pulled down to his eyes.

"Well?" Ogilvie said softly.

The boy's eyes darted around. He took out a cigarette and lit it, then took out the cards and began shuffling and reshuffling them.

"Coach made some last-minute changes," he said. "That's why I'm late."

"Give," Ogilvie said, keeping an eye on Engelberg, who seemed ready to flee at any moment.

"Well, his hat," the boy said, touching his own hat, "is now a bunt. When he touches his belt"—he reached for his own large silver one—"it means a steal. His ear"—he tugged at his earlobe—"means hit-and-run. And his nose"—he pinched his—"and shirt at the same time"—he brushed his fingers across his chest—"means squeeze play, when there's a runner on third."

"That it?" Ogilvie asked, making quick notes on a tiny piece of paper.

"That's all our signs."

Ogilvie peered around the woods carefully, then pulled a notebook out from under his shirt and removed several pages. He handed them to the Indian player.

The boy quickly leafed through the pages. "These can't be ALL your history notes, Ogilvie."

"Of course not," Ogilvie said calmly. "If your information pans out, you'll get the rest."

The boy nodded, rose, and dashed away through the woods.

Ogilvie and Engelberg nodded at each other, smiled, and walked slowly in the same direction.

The last Bears to arrive at the field were Amanda and Tanner, walking side by side. When they neared the dugout, Tanner broke away in a run up to Buttermaker.

"Coach! Coach!" he yelled happily. "Mandy can PITCH! She's OKAY!"

The Bears scrambled out of the dugout and surrounded Buttermaker, Tanner, and Amanda.

"How about it, Amanda?" Buttermaker asked.

"I'm okay," she said, her head down.

"You sure? It's only been a couple days since—"

"I said I'm okay."

"Well, maybe I should check with your—"

"I'm PITCHING!" She glared at him. "You don't need to check with NOBODY—uh, anybody."

"Well, okay, Amanda. But I'll be watching you closely. If you get tired, you're coming out."

Amanda struck out the Indian side in the first, then came to the dugout breathing heavily.

In the second, an Indian spanked a double down the left-field line, but was out trying to stretch it into a triple when Regi Tower missed the throw-in from left, but Tanner, alertly backing up the play, pounced on the ball and dove to tag the sliding runner.

Amanda labored through the next three innings, walking five, allowing three more hits, but managing to get crucial strikeouts.

The Bears' bats, meanwhile, were silent.

The Bears were hitting—or, more accurately, NOT hitting, but at bat—in the fourth when Kelly Leak appeared at the steps of the dugout.

"Where you been, Kelly?" Buttermaker asked, eyeing him stonily.

"I was, uh, I got tied up on some, uh, business, couldn't—"

"We could have used the last couple of games, kid. We could have used you today. If we don't win this one, we can kiss our chances good-bye."

Kelly glanced at the scoreboard, which still registered *Indians—0, Bears—0*. He smiled and held out his arms. "Well, here I am, Coach."

"You're too late, Kelly. We're going with what we have out there."

Kelly took a step backward, stunned. "You mean I can't play?"

"Not today, no."

"Okay, then." He turned and started to walk away. "You can all SHOVE IT!"

"You leave now, Kelly," Buttermaker said softly, "then don't come back."

Kelly stopped.

"Have a seat, Kelly," Buttermaker said.

Kelly pushed open a spot beside Amanda, then sat down and ignored her.

Between innings, several of the Bears grunted greetings to Kelly, who sat sulking on the bench.

In the bottom of the fifth, Ahmad beat out a bunt. Tanner got an infield single. Then the Indians' pitcher walked two straight Bears, forcing in a run.

In the last inning, with the Bears ahead 1–0, Amanda, throwing hard and sweating heavily, ran the count on the first batter to three balls and two strikes. Then, wincing as she threw, she broke off a sharp curve, which the batter missed by three feet, for her eighth strikeout.

The next batter connected solidly on the first pitch and sent a line triple over Toby Whitewood's head in center.

Amanda carefully mixed her pitches on the new batter, again running the count to three-and-two.

Ogilvie, leaning out of the dugout, was watching the Indians' third-base coach. Suddenly he grabbed Buttermaker's arm. "A bunt!" he whispered. "They're gonna try a SQUEEZE, Coach, the old SQUEEZE PLAY!"

"How do you know?" asked Buttermaker testily.

"From scouting, Coach, I'm SURE!"

Buttermaker called for timeout from the umpire and walked out to the mound, joined by Engelberg and the rest of the infield. Amanda's chest heaved with exhaustion, and she wiped her forehead with her glove.

"They may be trying a squeeze play," Buttermaker said quietly, "to bunt the runner home."

Amanda and Engleberg nodded.

"So just be on your toes, infield. You okay, Amanda?"

"You kidding? I could pitch a YEAR."

Buttermaker walked back to the dugout.

Amanda surveyed the situation carefully, checking the runner at third, then eyeing the batter and Engelberg's mitt-target. She threw a perfect half-speed strike. The batter bunted down the first-base line as the runner broke for the plate.

But Jose, already just a few feet from the plate, grabbed the ball with his bare hand, tagged the batter going by, and tossed quickly underhand to Engelberg, who, blocking the plate with his big body, slammed the tag on the sliding runner.

"OUT! BOTH OUT!" shouted the umpire, hooking his thumb into the air.

The victorious Bears romped to the pitcher's mound, hugging one another, throwing their gloves into the air. They lifted Ogilvie and carried him off the field.

CHAPTER 8

The ballet studio rattled with loud music from the accompanying piano as an overweight woman pirouetted gracelessly and leaped here and there, landing with great THUNKS on the floor.

She finished, and it was Amanda's turn.

"Go get 'em, Mandy," Engelberg said, gnawing on a chicken leg.

"Do it like on TV," said Ahmad, "all that twirling and stuff."

"Curves," said Tanner, "they're suckers for curve balls."

The three, seated on spectators' chairs, giggled as Amanda, red-faced, took the floor to dance. The music started, and Amanda looped her arms over her head and rose shakily onto her toes.

With a crash, Ogilvie burst into the studio, knocking over a chair and colliding with the other dancer, sending her careening into a wall-length mirror, which shivered but held.

"THE WHITE SOX BEAT THE METS! THE

WHITE SOX BEAT THE METS!" Ogilvie screamed, sending chairs and dancers skidding in various directions as he fought his way to his teammates. "THE WHITE SOX BEAT THE METS!" He sent one woman sprawling over the practice bar. " 'Scuse me, ma'am. HEY, I JUST CAME FROM THE FIELD—"

"Would you PLEASE—" The ballet teacher hopped across the studio toward Ogilvie on her toes.

"YAHOO!" shouted Tanner.

"MAN OH MAN!" yelled Ahmad.

"Ish IMPOSHIBLE!" belched Engelberg, his mouth full of chicken.

The three jumped up and hugged one another, dancing around in a circle.

Ogilvie scrambled up from the chair over which he had fallen onto his stomach and ran over to them, pursued by the teacher on her toes.

"GENTLEMEN, PLEASE—"

"It's true," Ogilvie said, panting for breath. "I just came from the field. The White Sox beat the Mets, 2–1."

"HOOORAH!" Amanda took a flying leap into the bunch, and they all tumbled to the floor in a jumble of arms, legs, chairs, and the ballet teacher.

"Gentlemen, Amanda, PLEASE—" The teacher grunted as she struggled to crawl out from under the pile.

"Then that means—" Engelberg said.

"That we're all alone—" Ahmad said.

"In SECOND PLACE!" said Tanner.

"IF we beat the Athletics tomorrow," said Ogilvie. Their spirits took a dip.

"Yeah, they're tough," said Ahmad.

"We just barely beat them LAST time," Tanner said.

"And that was with KELLY'S HITTING," Amanda said.

"Yeah," Engelberg said.

They all looked at each other.

"Oh my STARS!" groaned the ballet teacher. "Please get off my foot."

"But we'll BEAT them!" Tanner said, rousing them again.

"SURE!" Ahmad said.

"I would say our chances are at LEAST fifty-fifty," Ogilvie said.

"I'll fast-ball 'em, curve 'em, slider 'em, and SPIT-TER 'em!" Amanda said.

"And then we'll play the YANKEES for the CHAMPIONSHIP!" Tanner bellowed.

"And we'll BLASH 'EM OUTTA the PARSH!" yelled Engelberg, wolfing down the last of the chicken.

"But first," said Ogilvie, raising an index finger high out of the pile, "the Athletics."

"Right," they all said.

They unscrambled themselves and got to their feet, pulling the ballet teacher up with them. They began circling the studio in a conga line, pushing the teacher in front of them.

"Boomba, boomba, boom—BA! Boomba, boomba, boom—BA!"

"Please, gentlemen, PLEASE!" the teacher pleaded mournfully, tiptoeing at the head of the line in the grip of Tanner.

"Okay," Amanda said, breaking away. "All you turkeys get outta here. I got my lesson."

The boys split up and headed for the door, the teacher right behind them, waving her finger. "I will not STAND for this! I shall report this to the AUTHORI-

TIES! We will not allow such HOOLIGANS to disrupt our—"

"Hey, teacher," Tanner said, turning to face her at the door. "You better teach Mandy GOOD, or we'll be BACK!" They ran out laughing.

Buttermaker worried a lot about the game with the Athletics, and not only because the Athletics were a good, solid team. He feared that his Bears were looking past the Athletics toward a playoff with the Yankees.

And so, he had the Bears out at the field a half-hour early before the game for extra fielding practice.

His concern about overconfidence was not unfounded, because as soon as the Bears saw that Kelly Leak had rejoined the team for sure, and would play, and that Amanda was feeling fine, they begun strutting around like cocky roosters.

"Hey, give me something MEAN down here, Coach!" Tanner called from shortstop.

Buttermaker slapped a sharp, skidding grounder at Tanner. Tanner swopped his glove quickly under the ball and straightened up to throw. But the ball wasn't in his glove. Tanner examined the glove front and back. The ball was in left field. He laughed.

"Come on now, you guys," Buttermaker yelled out plaintively, "Look ALIVE! Be ready, Ahmad."

He lofted a high, lazy fly to right. Ahmad drifted under it, patting the pocket of his glove. Then, at the last instant, he spun and tried to catch it behind his back, getting it instead on the top of his head.

He rubbed his head with a smile as he picked up the ball and tossed it back in.

Buttermaker stood leaning on the bat, scowling.

"Don't worry, Coach," Ahmad called with a wave of his hand. "I won't be trying that in the game."

"HEY, BEARS!" Buttermaker hollered. "How you play now is how you'll play in a few minutes against the Athletics! Let's get it TOGETHER! Ready now . . ."

He tapped a bunt out in front of the plate. Engelberg whipped off his mask and pounced on it. But he didn't throw quickly. He first went into a full, slow pitcher's windup, then sent a knuckleball toward Jose, at first.

Jose, doubled up with laughter at Engleberg's flabby antics, felt the ball whoosh by, just grazing his luckily lowered head. "Dammit!" Buttermaker growled under his breath. "Okay, center, on your toes!" He lined a ball toward Toby Whitewood. Toby scooped it out of the air deftly, but he didn't throw it back to the infield.

"Let's chuck it around, Bears!" he shouted, tossing it underhand to Timmy Lupus, who was standing nearby looking at the stands and picking his nose. The ball hit him softly in the belly.

Timmy looked around to see who had punched him.

"Ball, Timmy!" Buttermaker called. "Pick up the ball!"

Timmy picked it up and looked at it.

Tanner ran out to take the ball from him, just as Timmy turned and heaved toward home. Tanner slid on his rump to avoid getting beaned.

The ball finally arrived at Buttermaker. He flipped it up and down, glaring at the Bears. "Kelly," he barked, "let's see if YOU can handle one!"

He lined one high and deep to left. Kelly turned and raced for the fence, taking it neatly over his shoulder. Then he spun and fired beautifully back to the plate on one hop.

Buttermaker sighed with relief. He looked over at Amanda, warming up with Ogilvie in front of the dugout. He noticed that she winced occasionally.

"How's it feel, Amanda?"

"Fine. I'm ready."

"Okay, Bears, get one!" He bounced a chopper to Regi Tower, at third. Regi backed up a few steps, then changed his mind and charged. His cap flew off as the ball bounced into his chest, knocking him onto his rear. The ball popped up and landed a few feet away in his upside-down cap.

Tanner was convulsed with laughter. "Hey, Coach, that count? He caught it, in a way!"

Buttermaker exhaled a long sigh and shook his head. "Okay, Bears," he said with resignation, "bring it in."

As the Bears filed into the dugout, Buttermaker stopped Kelly and took him aside. "Listen, Kelly," he said privately, "I want you handling the ball as much as possible today."

Kelly looked at him questioningly.

"That's right," Buttermaker said, "I want you to take everything you can get to. This is too darned important a game. Anything you can reach, catch. I don't want the others messing things up."

Kelly shrugged his shoulders and went to the dugout.

Buttermaker briefly scanned the stands. They were nearly full for this crucial game. The Agilars were there, of course, on their feet cheering even before the game began. Mr. Tower was there, looking a bit ridiculous in a Bears' cap a few sizes too small. Councilman Whitewood was there, looking right and left for somebody to shake hands with. Ahmad's brothers were there, chatting together calmly. Even Mr. Ogilvie was there, straining forward to peer through his thick glasses. And Mrs. Lupus was sitting primly, her purse in her lap. Roy Turner sat with Pigtails, jabbing her with an elbow once in a while and laughing.

"PLAY BALL!" the umpire shouted, dusting off the plate and pulling on his mask.

Buttermaker hurriedly called his team together. "Boys, I don't have to remind you what this game means to us. But I will anyway. It means we will be playing in the championship game against the Yankees. If we win. If we win. And what does that mean to the Athletics today? Ahmad, what does it mean?"

Ahmad flashed a wide, toothy grin. "It means a whole lot of BAAAD NEWS for the ATHLETICS!"

"BAD NEWS for the ATHLETICS!" the team echoed together as they burst out of the dugout to take the field.

Amanda put two fast balls past the leadoff batter, then struck him out with a roundhouse curve. She rubbed her elbow as the Bears pegged it around.

The second batter tapped an easy ground ball to Jose, who fumbled it, picked it up, and stepped on first.

The third batter hit a little pop fly to deep short. Tanner backpedaled under it. He bumped into Kelly Leak, who reached over his head to make the catch.

Tanner turned to look at him, but Kelly continued straight into the dugout.

"Hey, shortstop," said one of the Athletics as he passed Tanner on the way out, "does Kelly Leak go to the bathroom for you too?"

Tanner whirled around, but Regi grabbed him and pulled him along to the bench.

The Bears went down in order in the bottom of the first; so did the Athletics in the top of the second.

In the bottom of the second, the Bears scored a run. Kelly doubled to left-center, went to third on a wild pitch, and scored on Ahmad's bunt down the first-base line.

Both sides went down in order in the third. But there was grumbling in the Bears' dugout because, to get the third Athletic out, Kelly had raced in from left field and elbowed Regi away to catch a pop-up foul off third. Kelly sat silently with his head down.

The first two Athletics lined hard singles off Amanda in the next inning. Buttermaker knelt on one knee just outside the dugout, watching her carefully. The next two hitters struck out on slow pitches. Then a sizzling grounder was smashed down the third-base line past Regi's outstretched glove. But Kelly, playing in close, fielded the ball just behind the infield and rifled a strike to Jose to nip the batter by an eyelash.

Two Yankee players, spectators for this game, strolled past the Bears' dugout and looked in. "Hey, Leak," one said, "you should be playing all nine positions."

"Yeah," said the other one, "the other babies keep getting in your way."

They continued on, laughing and elbowing each other, as the Bears sat stiffly and Kelly stared at the ground.

Tanner gritted his teeth in quiet rage. "First he don't show up for two games. Then he comes back and thinks he's the whole team!"

Entering the last inning, the Bears still held on to their 1–0 lead.

The first Athletic ripped a double down the right-field line.

Buttermaker went to the mound. "What's the trouble?" he asked Amanda.

"Arm's stiffening," she said, rubbing her elbow. "Got nothing on the fast ball, curve ain't breaking."

"Want to come out?"

"Naw." She bent down and picked up the resin bag, tossed it a couple of times, and dropped it. "I got enough for three more outs."

"Sure?"

" 'Course."

"Well, stick to the corners, and keep it low. Just go for control."

Buttermaker went back to the dugout.

The next batter hit a towering fly ball to right-center. Ahmad, playing a shade toward center for the right-handed batter, was under it. But Kelly dashed from left to take it one-handed over Ahmad's head.

"Hey!" Ahmad glanced into the stands, then over at Kelly, who was walking back toward left. "What you doing, man?"

"Sorry," Kelly said softly, looking back over his shoulder. "I—"

"We got nine players on this team, you know."

Kelly shrugged.

Slowly and carefully picking the corners and keeping the pitches low, Amanda struck out the next batter.

With two outs and a runner still on second, the batter hoisted a fly to deep center. Toby Whitewood backed up under it. Kelly trotted over beside him, but then made no attempt to take it. Toby, distracted by Kelly, muffed the catch. The tying run scored. The Athletic bench went wild with cheering, while the Bears stood silently. Amanda ran the count to three-and-two on the batter. Then he swung and tipped it foul, right back into Engelberg's mitt. Engelberg hung on, surprised, for the final out of the inning.

As the Bears came to the dugout, Buttermaker pulled Kelly aside. "What the devil were you doing out there on that last one?" he growled softly. "I gave you instructions which I expect to be followed."

Kelly shrugged.

"Come on." Buttermaker tapped him on his rear. "You lead off. Grab a bat and get down to business."

Kelly sullenly picked up a bat and walked listlessly up to the plate. Although the Bears' rooters in the stands were alive with yelling, no cheers of encouragement followed Kelly from the bench.

Kelly let the first pitch go by for a strike without moving his bat, then swung halfheartedly and missed the second.

Buttermaker trotted out and called for time. He put his arm around Kelly and gripped his shoulder hard with his fingers. "What in blazes is going on with you?" he whispered.

Kelly looked at him coldly.

"You want to win this game or not?"

Kelly looked over at the silent dugout. Most of the Bears sat back in the shadows. Ogilvie and Lupus knelt forward, staring out expectantly, their faces sweaty.

Amanda bounced up. "Come on, Bears!" she shouted. "Talk it up like a TEAM! Let's get a HIT!"

A few grunted.

Kelly pulled away from Buttermaker's grasp. "Just let me alone to bat, Coach."

Buttermaker walked away and crouched nervously outside the dugout.

Kelly blasted the next pitch over the scoreboard in center for a homer to win the game.

Spectators rushed onto the field. Kelly rounded the bases and was greeted exultantly at home plate by Ogilvie, Lupus, Amanda, and Buttermaker.

The rest of the team languished quietly near the bench, showing light smiles as they received praise from their relatives and friends. Buttermaker was quickly surrounded by admiring parents who clapped him on the back and shook his hand.

". . . On your way now . . ." "for the championship . . ." "wouldn't have believed it . . ." "take those

Yankees EASY . . ." "some player, that Leak . . ." "manager of the year in a WALK . . ." "out of nowhere . . ." "you're a magician, Buttermaker . . ." "fine bunch of players . . ."

By the time Buttermaker had extricated himself from the fans, the team had dispersed.

Kelly straddled his motorcycle near the bicycle rack, where the Bears were gathered. "Hey," he said, "anybody want Cokes, on me?"

Ogilvie and Lupus said, "Sure." Amanda nodded and looked at the rest of the Bears. They were already on their bikes, and they pedalled away in groups of two and three.

Distant thunder rumbled in the night sky as Buttermaker pulled into the parking lot by the field. He stared pensively into the distance, musing about the prospects for the championship game the next day.

It was some time before he noticed the shadowy figure seated on the pitcher's mound. It was Roy Turner. Buttermaker got out and walked over.

Turner took a swig from a bottle of Scotch and sang, "Take me out to the ball . . . game, take me out with the crowd. Buy me some peanuts and—"

"What time did the bar open here, Turner?" Buttermaker said.

Turner looked up. "Hey, there, old Buttermaker, old friend, Buttermaker, you old ballplayer, you." He took another long drink from the bottle, and set it down on the pitching rubber beside him. He reached for a glove and ball that lay nearby. "Come on, old man, less fling a few."

Buttermaker waved his hand and sat down beside Turner. "Never throw the day before a game," he said. "Bad luck."

"Aaaw, wha's the difference? We're jus' a couple ole men playin' with kids. Here"—he handed the bottle to Buttermaker—"take a drink, on me."

"No thanks. I don't drink."

"Don' DRINK? Haaw! You drink like a FISH, Buttermonger. I rememer one time I hadda CARRY YOU INSIDE, you was so sloshed."

"Not anymore, Roy. You go ahead."

Turner drank. "Nineteen years," he said, shaking his head. "Tha's a long time, nineteen years . . ."

"What's the trouble?"

"Trouble? Tha's my middle name. Roy Trouble Turner. Tha's me." He took another drink.

"What's the trouble on this particular occasion?"

"On this particlar occasion, my ole friend, my wife wants a divorce. She wants me outta the house."

Buttermaker pursed his lips. "Sorry to hear that."

"Aaaw, it aini't so bad. Nineteen good years. Raised a good boy. Joey'll be a good one, Butterbaker. Strong, fast. I coached Eddie Wakely too, memmer him? Star in college now. I coached him good."

"You're a good coach, Turner."

Turner took a long drink and choked a bit, coughing. "Good coach, tha's a laugh. Nineteen years." He chuckled. "My wife don't want me as a coach on her team no more."

A light rain began to fall. The two men sat silently, staring at home plate.

"You think I'm a jerk, don't you, Butterbaker?"

"Sometimes, Turner, not always."

"Yeah, I am. Too harsh. Too harsh on the boys, on my boy. Too harsh on my wife. But I do some good aroun' here, don't I? Hunh?" He looked appealingly at Buttermaker, who nodded.

"Yeah, I do. Anyway, it's what I do best, coach

baseball. It's all I know how to do. She doesn't unnerstand that. Why in heck should she? And she's right, nashurly. She's ALWAYS right."

"Not necessarily," Buttermaker said.

"Wouldn't you please have a li'l drink with me?"

"Okay." Buttermaker took the bottle. "With you, I'll have a little drink."

"Thanks," Turner said.

The rain pelted down harder, dripping off the bills of their baseball caps.

"I think," Buttermaker said hesitantly, "that you and Jill should talk more."

"She don' wanna talk."

"Not about the Yankees, maybe. About yourselves."

Turner turned to look at him. "Yeah, maybe tha's right. I only talk about the Yankees. I got nothin' else to talk about. Nothin' 'bout me is innersting enough to talk about. But you know, it's hard to look back at all this and say iss all foolish. You think iss all foolish, don't you, all this baseball crap."

"No," Buttermaker said, "I don't."

"Yeah," Turner said, "it is." He stared into the dark and the pouring rain. "Iss much more important for peoble to get along with each other than for peoble to go roun' tryin' to beat each other. Peoble got to, uh, you know, I think about . . . sometimes I get . . . tryin' to figger out wha's important and not important . . . and wha's it all about. You unnerstan what I mean, Buttermaker?"

"Yeah." Buttermaker nodded. "Maybe we should be going. We got a big game tomorrow, and—"

"Like, wha's important and wha's not . . ." Tears started to roll down Turner's face, and he turned away in embarrassment. Suddenly he stiffened. "HEY!"

Buttermaker jumped.

"The FEEELD! Butterbacker, our goldarn field is gettin' SOAKED! The goldarn INFIELD!"

Turner stumbled to his feet and ran unevenly toward the rolled-up tarpaulins beside the dugout, Buttermaker right behind him.

They struggled and strained to roll out the tarps over the infield, sweat mixing with the rain on their faces.

"We mussa been SLEEPIN', Butteraker, this coulda been a SWAMP," Turner said, groaning with effort, and slipping to his knees occasionally. "Our goldarn champaship game coulda got CANCELED."

He slipped and fell. Buttermaker helped him up. Finally the field was covered. Turner stood, swaying, on the tarp. Buttermaker reached out to steady him. Turner pushed him away.

"Big champaship game tomorrow," Turner said.

"Right."

"Well, I got a li'l secret for you, Butteraker. We gonna whomp crap outta you tomorrow."

"Come on, Roy, I'll take you home."

Turner pushed him away again, smiling. "Whomp the be-Jesus outta your li'l Bearsies."

"We'll both be tough, Turner," Buttermaker said, smiling back.

"Yeah. Ill be the toughess champiship game in the hissry of the league. I don't need no help. You go on. I'll be awright." Turner sloshed away through the puddles. "See you on the FEEL OF PLAY, BEARS!"

Buttermaker watched him lurch away toward the parking lot, his feet splashing spray to both sides. Buttermaker shook his head and headed for his Cadillac.

"Just relax, Kelly," Amanda said, "it'll be okay. We're doing the right thing. He ain't gonna do nuthin' to you OR me. I ain't never seen a man yet that could stand up to a woman wanting to be friends."

The front door opened and shut. Kelly shivered slightly.

His father came into the room and stopped short upon seeing the two. His eyes flashed fire as he looked them up and down, without speaking.

Amanda nudged Kelly. "Uh, Dad," Kelly said, "uh, I'd like you to meet my friend, uh, Amanda Whurlizer."

"Glad to meet you, Mr. Leak," Amanda said, smiling and sticking out her hand.

"Mmph," Mr. Leak grunted shyly as they shook hands.

"I just wanted you to meet her, Dad," Kelly said, his words tumbling out. "She's a great pitcher, really good, and a wonderful person, and you oughta see her in the championship game tomorrow."

"I told you I didn't want you playin' no baseball," Mr. Leak muttered, in a tone more grumpy than angry.

"And not to see Amanda anymore, remember?" Kelly said, chancing a smile.

"Mmph." Mr. Leak's face turned crimson.

"But I wanted you to see for yourself how nice she is. I ain't been in trouble once since Amanda and me started hanging out together."

Mrs. Leak came into the room. She started immediately to back out. Kelly took her arm and introduced her to Amanda. She looked anxiously at her husband, who was staring away from all of them. Then, without smiling, she cautiously, briefly, took Amanda's hand, still looking at her husband.

"Why don't you come out to the game tomorrow, Ma?" Kelly said. "It'll be a great game. Amanda will be pitching, and—"

"She ain't goin' outta this house," Mr. Leak mumbled. "She don't need to see no game."

Kelly looked at the floor and bit his lip.

"But I might," his father said, in a voice so low as to barely be heard. "I might come out, if I feel like it."

Around town, members of the North Valley League Bears tossed and turned in their beds, their eyes springing open occasionally, then closing slowly again, as they played and replayed the next day's championship game over and over in their minds, imagining all sorts of heroics and disasters.

Coach Buttermaker sat staring at the television test-pattern, playing and replaying in his mind not the upcoming game, but a dozen games from years ago, not imagining heroics and disasters, but recalling them, his moods soaring and plummeting in a traumatic concert of memories of his baseball career.

The only Bear to sleep soundly that night was Mike Engelberg, who, because he had been starving himself for the previous few days, had gorged himself on a pregame feast of steak, spaghetti, apple pie, and a peanut-butter-and-olive sandwich so as to be sure he had a sufficient supply of energy for the final effort.

CHAPTER 9

Championship day dawned breezy, bright, clear, and warm. The crowd began to form early at North Valley League Field.

And one of the first things seen by the early spectators—and only the early ones—was a small, hand-painted banner that fluttered above Old Glory on the center-field flagpole. The banner read: YANKEES ARE CRUDS.

Pigtails raced to the flagpole and brought the offending banner down.

A half-hour before game time, the parking lot, snack bar, and bleachers were all jammed with happy, excited fans and players. Councilman Whitewood, wearing a Bears cap and baseball shoes, busied himself carrying supplies to the snack bar.

The Yankees warmed up slowly in front of their dugout, along the third-base line; the Bears warmed up in front of their dugout, along first.

In the Bears dugout was a somber scene. Amanda soaked her arm in a big bucket of hot water. Ogilvie poured in Epsom salts. From time to time she lifted her arm out so Buttermaker could massage it.

"Hurt a lot?" he asked.

"I'll make it," she said, gritting her teeth as he rubbed her elbow.

Ogilvie produced a ream of paper. "Want to go over the scouting reports again, Mandy?"

"Naw. What we don't know by now we'll never know."

Councilman Whitewood came down the steps with a fresh bucket of steaming water and substituted it for the old one. Amanda immediately plunged her arm in.

What wouldn't be noticeable to the crowd in the stands watching the Bears warm up was all too apparent to Buttermaker. There was tension beyond that of pre-game jitters. Kelly Leak was getting the cold shoulder.

Several baseballs went back and forth, but none was thrown to Kelly. He motioned for the ball from Jose, but Jose threw to Miguel. Kelly moved over toward Tanner and Ahmad and held up his glove. But Tanner threw to Ahmad. Kelly watched them throw back and forth a few times, then reached in and intercepted the ball. "Anybody mind if I warm up?" he said.

Tanner spat on the grass. "We didn't think you needed anybody but yourself to play catch with," he said acidly.

Buttermaker was watching this while he massaged Amanda's arm.

"Hi, Mo."

Buttermaker snapped his head around. Amanda's sister, Brenda, was standing at the corner of the dugout. Buttermaker jumped up and went over to her. "Hello," he said.

"I came to see Amanda pitch," she said.

"Good, I'm glad. She's great. A little sore today, though, hope she'll be okay."

"After the game," Brenda said, "would you like to have a drink?"

Buttermaker smiled. "Coke," he said.

"Coke is fine," Brenda said, smiling back. "See you later."

He watched her walk away toward the stands, and was suddenly filled with a deep sense of comfort and satisfaction that he hadn't known in years. He was surprised at the joy that swept over him, the pleasure of being surrounded by his team, with Brenda nearby. He had never felt so complete.

Then he went back to Amanda.

Meanwhile, Tanner and Kelly had been glaring at each other.

"Just cool it, Tanner," Kelly said.

"You wanna play catch, Leak? Hunh?" Tanner walked up to him. "Try catching THIS!" He swung a right, grazing Kelly's chin, and they grabbed each other and wrestled to the ground, raising a cloud of dust. Other Bears instantly gathered around. Jimmy Feldman, trying to hold his face away to protect his recently healed nose, reached in to break them apart, but other players pulled him back, making an aisle for Buttermaker, who plunged in on top of the two fighters.

He separated them, holding each by his collar. "What's this garbage?" he asked, looking from one to the other. Neither answered. They stood panting, wiping dirt off their faces, sneering at each other.

"Well?" Buttermaker asked insistently.

"Kelly's a crud," Tanner said, spitting.

"It's because Kelly's been hogging the ball," Lefty said, "and we're all sick of it."

179

"Yeah," said Ahmad, "he's not the ONLIEST reason we got this far."

"Well, actually," Ogilvie said, raising his finger, "he IS most of the reason, along with—"

Tanner shoved Ogilvie, knocking him over backward. "Just shut UP!"

Amanda and Engelberg lifted Ogilvie up and dusted him off.

"Okay, cool down, Tanner," Buttermaker said, still holding him by his collar. "Now, guys, I don't think we have to—"

"If you guys played better," Amanda broke in, fuming, "Kelly wouldn't have to cover for you all the time!"

"No GIRL has to tell me how to play!" Tanner snapped.

"Oh YEAH?" Amanda snarled back.

"YEAH!" Tanner churned his feet, trying to escape Buttermaker's grasp.

Amanda leaned toward him, her fists clenched. "Let loose of this turkey, Buttermaker, and I'll chew his ears off and spit them right back in his FACE!"

"OH YEAH?"

"SHUT UP!" Buttermaker roared. "That's enough of this. You're acting like a bunch of babies."

"Well, we're sick of Kelly," said Toby, "acting like he's the only one on this team."

"Cool it, everybody," Kelly broke in. "Everybody can just relax about that. I won't be a problem no more, 'cause I'm quitting."

Buttermaker released Tanner and grabbed Kelly, spinning him around. "Hell if you're quitting! You came this far, you're going to finish. Just like"—he quickly looked around at the faces—"everybody else on this team. The truth is, you can all blame me for Kelly

180

making those plays yesterday. I ORDERED him to. So that's that."

The players looked at each other.

"But why, Coach?" Ahmad asked. "Why'd you do that?"

"But, Coach," Regi said, "we got all this way with everybody doing his share."

"Yeah," several boys said.

Buttermaker studied them, searching their eyes, confused, wishing Kelly would say something to help out. But he didn't.

"Okay," he said finally, "what's done is done. We got a big game. Let's cut out the nonsense and play it. We're going to pull out all the stops today, to win. And everybody's going to play. EVERYBODY."

He watched the team walk back to the dugout.

In the Yankees dugout, the scene was much different. Roy Turner stood before his seated players, looking gravely from one somber face to the next. They were attentive, as always.

"Boys, you are the defending champions. You own the title. And today you will be defending it against a bunch of beginners who don't even belong on the same field with you. But they'll be trying to take your title away. Just like . . ." His mind wandered briefly. ". . . people will always try to do, all your life.

"So you have to be ready to defend what's yours, to hold on to your titles, like champions . . ." He thought of Jill, who again was there in her seat behind the dugout to support him and the team. ". . . Like Yankees. And if I know Coach Buttermaker, we'll have to fight for this one every inch of the way."

Cheers and applause burst from the stands as the Bears took the field. Their uniforms were basically clean, but showed the wear and tatters and grass stains of their long and difficult season.

The Yankees, clean, neat, and tailored as usual, lined the front of their dugout as their first batter stepped to the plate, confidently swinging his bat to loosen up.

The Bears began a weak chatter behind Amanda. She delivered her first pitch.

It was banged sharply to left field for a base hit.

"Settle down, Amanda," Buttermaker called through his cupped hands.

Amanda shook her head and kicked the rubber. Her next pitch bounced in the dirt past Engelberg, and the runner took second.

Tanner trotted up to take the throw from Engelberg. He handed the ball to Amanda. "Get it together, Mandy."

"Honk it out your tailpipe, Tanner," Amanda said, kicking the dirt and eyeing the runner on second.

Several Yankees, now sensing the Bears' dissension, began to yell: "No pitcher out there . . ." "No TEAM out there . . ." "They ain't together, guys . . ." "They're not ready to play ball . . ." "Get 'em NOW, YANKEES . . ."

Amanda's next pitch was smashed off the left-field fence. Kelly raced after it. The Yankee runner rounded third and headed for the plate. Kelly's throw was a bullet. It hit the dirt just in front of the plate, skipping under Engelberg's glove.

Amanda, backing up the play, caught it and charged for the plate. The runner slid, feet high, his rubber cleats smacking into Amanda's chest. She dropped the ball and spun around in pain.

"SAFE!" the umpire bellowed.

Tanner was the first one there, kneeling beside

Amanda and putting a hand on her shoulder as she doubled over.

Buttermaker ran out, pointing to the Yankee who had scored and hollering to the ump: "You see what he did? Hey, you see what he did? He should be thrown out!"

The boy walked away, dusting himself off. "If she can't take it," he said, "she shouldn't be playing in a guy's game."

Tanner sprung to his feet and kicked the boy between the legs. The boy went down holding his groin.

Instantly, players poured out of both dugouts. Yankees swarmed over Tanner, arms, legs, fists flying. Kelly came tearing in from left field and piled into them, ripping Yankees off the top, throwing punches here and there. Buttermaker, Roy Turner, the umpire, and Pigtails finally separated the two teams.

The umpire directed both teams back to their dugouts and called a hasty conference with Buttermaker and Turner.

"I oughta call this whole thing off," the ump said angrily. "If you two coaches can't control your—"

"That high-foot slide was a cheap shot, Turner," Buttermaker barked. "Let's cut out that crap."

"It was meant as clean, hard baseball, Buttermaker," Turner said, with stern earnestness.

"It was barely legal," the umpire said, waggling a finger in Turner's face. Then he put his finger in Buttermaker's face. "As for you, I'LL call the plays. You keep your team in line."

The two coaches nodded and returned to their dugouts. The Bears retook the field. Buttermaker walked Amanda to the mound.

"You okay, babe?"

She rubbed her chest. "I ain't got much there," she said with a faint smile. "I'll be okay."

Kelly and Tanner walked out to their positions side by side.

"I didn't need your help, Kelly," Tanner said.

"I know."

Tanner glanced into the Yankee dugout. "They're all cruds."

"Yeah.

"Hope you go four-for-four," Tanner said, "we'll need it."

"I'll try."

The violent action galvanized the Bears, brought the team together. Now as they crouched, ready for action, they beat their small fists into their gloves and raised their voices in a babel of strong chatter behind Amanda.

She straightened her cap and pitched.

Miguel swatted down a hard grounder and threw the batter out. The team raved its approval as they pegged it around the infield.

Tanner, knocked over backward by a hard liner, held on for the out.

Cheers enveloped the Bears, and continued as Amanda struck out the next Yankee on three pitches.

Ahmad led off for the Bears. Joey Turner lobbed in easy pitches—as he liked to for most of the weak-hitting Bears—but took too much off the ball and missed the plate badly. Ahmad ducked as two soft ones went over his head, then took a third one wide.

"That's the old EYE, Ahmad," Buttermaker shouted, clapping his hands, "just one more now!"

But Ahmad swung and popped it up for the out.

"What are you doing, Ahmad," Buttermaker asked

184

angrily at the dugout, "swinging at a three-and-o pitch?"

"Well, it was right where I usually like 'em—"

"You almost had a walk. This is a team game, don't be selfish. Use your head up there."

Tanner grounded out. That brought up Kelly Leak.

Kelly strode to the plate accompanied by loud, expectant cheering from the stands and the bench, who were informed by the announcer that Leak now led the league in batting with an even .700 average. He stepped in and dug in his rear foot, swinging his hips to set himself, and staring out at Joey Turner.

Turner's first pitch was several feet outside.

"They're scared of ya, Kelly," Tanner yelled.

The second pitch was just as wide, and the cheers on the bench turned to boos, for it became quickly obvious that the Yankees were indeed scared of Kelly, and were going to walk him intentionally. The third pitch was wide, and the booing spread to the stands. Kelly slung his bat aside in disgust, and the umpire warned him not to do that again.

Ball four, Kelly trotted down to first.

Buttermaker huddled with Toby in the on-deck circle. "A lot of those soft pitches are coming way inside," Buttermaker said. "Lean into one of those and let it hit you."

"Hunh?" said Toby, with a worried look.

"We're pulling out all the stops. Engelberg's up after you, and he's been killing the ball lately. So just get on base. Do what I tell you, it's the safest way."

Toby stood nervously at the plate. He leaned in at the expected blooper ball and took a gentle hit on the arm, and was awarded first.

Engelberg stepped up with two runners on. He lashed one to the fence in left, scoring Kelly and Toby, and pulled up at second with a double. He thumbed his nose at Joey Turner, who kicked dirt around the mound.

Turner bore down and struck out Jose to end the inning.

At the end of one, the Bears led, 2–1.

Amanda walked to the mound, followed by jeers from the Yankee dugout. Two of the boys leaned out holding a pair of athletic supporters tied together with a string to resemble a weird bra. "Hey, pitcher!" one of them yelled, dangling it and waving it around, "Maybe ten years from now you'll need this!" The bench broke into laughter.

Amanda turned her back and faced right field, muttering to herself.

Toby took a fly ball in center for an out.

A ground ball was hit up the middle. Tanner dove and knocked it down, then scrambled to his feet and threw. Jose stretched to take the throw, but the umpire called, "Safe."

"Out by a mile!" Buttermaker yelled. "By a MILE!"

Amanda struck out the next batter, grimacing as she threw. Kelly took a fly in left to end the inning.

The first two Bears went out quickly. Regi started toward the plate.

"ATTACK that thing!" came the familiar shout from the crowd.

"Regi Tower is a sissy!" came a cry from the Yankee dugout.

White with anger, Regi swung viciously at three pitches, missing them all.

Both sides went down in order in the third.

To start the fourth, Tanner moved too slowly after a grounder, and the ball bounced off his glove for an error.

Buttermaker slammed his fist on his thigh as he paced the dugout. "Been telling him all season to put his body in front of it!"

Timmy and Ogilvie nodded somberly.

A ground ball was driven up the middle into center for a hit. Toby chased it down. The lead runner headed toward third, and rounded it. Jose ran in behind second to take the cutoff throw. But Toby threw all the way to the plate, too late to prevent the run, and allowing the batter to go to second, where he veered to knock over Jose violently in the process.

The Bears raged their protest at the foul by the runner, and in the stands the Agilars led the booing. The field umpire scolded the runner, who apologized.

Buttermaker, meanwhile, was screaming at Toby: "Throw to your CUTOFF MAN, not to the PLATE!"

The Bears got the side out with no further damage, but the score was tied, 2–2.

Amanda came into the dugout and immediately plopped her arm into the bucket of hot water and Epsom salts. Ogilvie moved over beside her. "Next inning," he said confidentially, "their leadoff batter loves them high and inside. Don't give him anything there."

"Got it," Amanda said.

Buttermaker called to Lefty Stein. Stein came over. "How's your wrist? Can you play?"

"Yeah, sure, I'm fine." Lefty flexed his wrist to demonstrate.

"Okay. I want you to hit for Toby, and play center field. Okay?"

"Yeah," Lefty said, nodding happily.

"Okay. Now, Joey Turner is really getting wild. Either let him walk you or let him hit you."

"Aaw," Lefty whined, "Toby already got hit once—"

"Listen, Lefty, we're still in this game. We need to

get a runner on. Don't try to swing." He sent him up to the plate with a whack on the butt.

Jimmy Feldman came over to Buttermaker. "Coach, you better take Amanda out, she's hurting pretty bad."

"I asked her," Buttermaker said, his mind on Lefty. "She said she wanted to stay in."

" 'Course she did, but I really think you should—"

"All right, Lefty, baby! Let's have a good eye up there!"

Lefty took a slow ball inside, but stepped away from it, shaking his head. Rather than take the next pitch, or be hit with it, he swung, topped a slow roller to the mound, and was thrown out.

"BLAST IT!" Buttermaker was furious, and became more so when Engelberg and Jose, trying to draw walks as he instructed, took called third strikes.

The Bears started to take the field, but Buttermaker called them back. "Everybody in the dugout! Move it!"

He ripped off his cap and dashed it to the ground. "Stein, you don't follow instructions and you'll find yourself right back here on the bench. And the rest of you, what in blazes is the matter! All season long you've been laughed at, crapped on. And now you've got a chance to spit it right back in their faces! But you're lying around out there like a bunch of dead fish! Mistakes! Bonehead plays! Not following instructions! When I say to let one of those feather-balls hit you, don't back away from it! When I say to draw walks, that doesn't mean to watch three strikes go by! You've gotta use your HEADS!"

He looked slowly down the row of seated Bears.

"But, Coach," came Ahmad's voice softly, "all we want to do is play regular baseball."

188

"Yeah," Regi said, also softly, "we just aren't up to fancy stuff, like taking certain pitches, getting hit . . ."

"We get confuse of the baseball," said Jose.

"But," said Buttermaker, a bit unnerved, "don't you want to WIN?"

"We just gotta play our best, Coach," Kelly said, "that's the only way we can win."

Buttermaker stared at his hands for a few moments.

The umpire walked over. "Hey, Coach, get your team on the field."

"Okay, okay." He nodded at the ump. He stood silently for a moment. He still had lessons to learn about people. But he was learning, learning faster. There was still time. "Okay, Bears, I get the message. Let's get out there and play good baseball."

The Bears took their positions, including Lefty Stein in center. Toby Whitewood sat disconsolately on the bench. Buttermaker knelt in front of him, took him by the shoulders, and looked him in the eyes.

"Look, Toby, I didn't take you out because of anything you did. I put Lefty in because everybody's got to have a chance to play in this game, like I said. Okay? Isn't that what this is all about? Isn't that why this team was formed?"

Toby wiped away a tear and smiled slightly. "Yeah, I forgot."

Buttermaker closed his eyes, ashamed of his half-truth to Toby. For the fact was, Lefty had a better arm, if his wrist was okay. That's why he was put in. Even as he tried desperately to learn, to correct his mistakes in dealing with the team, he felt he was handling too many things badly. He was trapped somehow into making an unending series of bad judgments, despite which the Bears had made it to this championship game. He was always trying to catch up to his team. He would keep trying. They would all make it. Not so far to go now . . .

His self-centered reverie was interrupted by Joey Turner's towering home-run blast over the center-field fence, putting the Yankees ahead, 3–2.

The Bears came to bat. Amanda quickly soaked her elbow for a couple of minutes. With one out, she went to the plate. She ran the count to three-and-two, not so much because she had a good eye, but because it hurt to swing.

Joey delivered the payoff pitch. Amanda thought it had the outside corner and started to swing, but the bat slid out of her hands.

"BALL FOUR!" the umpire called.

The catcher whirled to argue. Amanda breathed a sigh of relief as she took first.

The Yankees were expecting a bunt from Ahmad. He bunted down the third-base line, and the catcher ran it down and threw him out, but Amanda went to second. As she was dusting herself off from the slide, she took her foot off the bag, forgetting to call for timeout. The first-basemen threw to pick her off, but the shortstop covering second was busy ogling Amanda, and the ball went into center. Amanda went to third, sliding again, dusting herself off again, but keeping a foot solidly on the bag.

Miguel stepped in. He took two strikes. Amanda danced on and off the bag at third, distracting Joey Turner. He pitched two balls. Then, as Amanda feinted toward the plate, Joey threw wildly past the catcher and the backstop. Amanda raced home with the tying run.

The teams went into the last inning tied, 3–3.

The Bears were tired. They had a new assortment of bruises on their bodies and rips in their uniforms. Buttermaker regarded them apprehensively as they wearily picked up their gloves in the dugout. A bandaid hung loosely from Tanner's cheek, and Buttermaker put a new one on. Jose, having been run over on the base path earlier, limped badly, and he rubbed his knee, over which spread a purple bruise.

"Jose," Buttermaker said, "you better sit down. Jimmy Feldman, you ready?"

"Yeah, Coach, yeah."

"Okay, you play first base. Regi Tower, you take a rest. Ahmad, you play third." He put his arm around Regi's shoulders. "Good game, Regi. Lupus? Timmy?"

Timmy, seated on the far end of the bench watching the Yankees swing bats, looked up.

"I want you in there for the last inning, Timmy. Take Ahmad's place in right."

Heads turned toward Timmy, then toward Buttermaker.

"But, Coach," Ogilvie said, "we still have a CHANCE."

"A darn GOOD chance, Ogilvie. And I'm gonna want you in there too in a few minutes."

"I can't play," Ogilvie gasped, his face turning blue, "can't breathe, my asthma . . ."

As the Bears dragged themselves out of the dugout, Buttermaker turned away from Ogilvie just in time to see Amanda, trying to conceal her movements at the end of the dugout, slip her fingers into a jar of Vaseline and rub them under the bill of her cap.

He edged over to her. "Amanda?"

She hid the jar.

"Don't try it, Amanda," he said, putting a hand gently on her shoulder. "A spitter's not the answer to—"

"Butt out." She shook his hand off, put on her cap, and stalked out to the mound.

Timmy stopped next to Buttermaker, his head down. "Don't send me in," he said softly. "I want us to win this game more than I want to play."

Buttermaker put a hand on his shoulder. "You didn't come into this life to sit around on benches all day, did you?" No answer. "Well then"—Buttermaker propelled him forward with a slap on his rump—"get your tail into right field."

Timmy trotted off reluctantly, pausing every few steps to look back at the bench.

In the stands, Mrs. Lupus, seeing Timmy enter the game, stood and clapped her hands. The Agilars cheered loudly. Councilman Whitewood sprang from his seat and headed down toward the field.

An announcement came over the P.A.: "Parents and friends. This is the last inning of our league championship game. It has been a wonderful and exciting season. How about giving a big hand for these little people who made it all possible!"

Everyone rose and applauded.

Councilman Whitewood appeared at the Bears' dugout. His face was pinched with concern. He stood close beside Buttermaker, and spoke in a near whisper. "Is it really necessary to put that Lupus kid in now?"

Buttermaker kept his eyes on the field. "He hasn't played yet."

"Yeah, old chum, I understand that, but we're still in this game, could win it. Don't you think you should go with the best—"

His voice was lost among shouts and screams as Amanda's pitch was rapped into right field, hitting in front of Timmy and rolling a few feet past him. By the time he threw it back in, the runner had reached second.

"For heaven's SAKE, Buttermaker!" Whitewood whispered hoarsely, rubbing his mouth in anguish.

"He's finishing the game, Bob," Buttermaker said, still not looking at him.

Whitewood, up to then disguising the nature of the conversation by appearing relaxed to anyone watching from the stands, now lost his temper. He grabbed Buttermaker's arm. "Listen, you! Don't give me your righteous nonsense! Winning this game is the only thing that can save these boys after all they went through this season. You're trying to play God to these little idiots, instead of just helping them win the damn GAME!"

Buttermaker turned slowly toward Whitewood, took the man's shirt collar firmly in his fist, and shoved him slowly but strongly step by step down into the dugout. "Whitewood," he said calmly, twisting the collar tightly, "you started this business supposedly to give these boys a chance to play baseball. That was a nice idea. I intend to carry it out."

Whitewood's face grew white from the choking tension of Buttermaker's grip on his collar.

"Now then," Buttermaker went on, still speaking calmly, "get yourself back in the stands where you belong before I carry out an idea of my own, which is to stuff my fist in your ear."

Whitewood stumbled away, his eyes wide and staring.

Buttermaker turned back to field to see Amanda grimace with pain as she threw a pitch into the dirt. He signaled for timeout from the umpire and trotted out to the mound.

Amanda spoke before he had a chance to. "Just three more outs, suds-head, hunh? I know I can do it. I . . ." She rubbed her fingers under the bill of her cap. "I can pull out all the stops . . ."

He shook his head and patted her shoulder. "The

team has to come first, Amanda. Your arm is shot. You've brought us a long way, babe." He looked out toward center. "Stein!" He waved him in.

The rest of the infield gathered around Amanda and Buttermaker. She blushed. "You're making a mistake, Coach," she said softly, " 'cause I got just enough to . . ." Tears formed in her eyes.

Tanner pushed through to Amanda. "Look, you crud. You did everything you could. Now knock it off and help us win."

She handed the ball to Buttermaker, who handed it to Lefty. She started to walk toward the dugout, her shoulders sagging pathetically. Buttermaker stopped her.

"You'll have to play center, Amanda."

She nodded, brightened a bit at being able to stay in the game, and trotted out to center field. She received loud applause from the stands and cheers from the Bears.

In the stands, Councilman Whitewood grumbled to those sitting around him: "What a dumb move, bringing in that Stein kid."

The Bears set themselves in position and picked up their weary chatter behind their new pitcher.

Lefty's first pitch was rifled on the ground back up through the middle, past the outstretched gloves of the diving Tanner and Miguel. Two walks loaded the bases.

Buttermaker knelt in front of the dugout, staring with narrowed eyes.

A chopper bounced toward Tanner at short, took a bad hop off a pebble, and smashed into his face, then rolled into left field. Kelly sprang after it, but two runs scored. Tanner shook his head and wiped away a dribble of blood from his nose.

From the Yankee side, the cheers were deafening; from the Bears' stands, there was silence.

Lefty got the next batter to pop up to Miguel. The Bears pepped up their chatter a little.

A one-bouncer was smacked at third. Ahmad speared it, dropping to his knees, but recovered too late to make the throw. Another run scored, making it 6–3.

The Yankees were all out in front of their dugout, cheering ecstatically over the big inning.

A fly went to center. Amanda took it cleanly, but her limp arm was useless for throwing to the plate. The runner took advantage of the weak toss in and scored from third after tagging up. Amanda turned her back to the diamond and swiftly wiped tears away.

With runners on first and second, the batter lined a sharp single to left. Kelly charged it and fired perfectly to the plate, holding the runners to an advance only to second and third.

The next batter sliced one to the mound. Lefty bobbled it and stumbled to his knees. Tanner raced in to pick it up, but too late to prevent another run.

Buttermaker knelt rock-still, but his jaw quivered with tension.

Lefty stared in at Engelberg's mitt, his chest heaving as he tried to regain his breath and control. Finally he wound up and threw. The pitch was belted deep to right. The Bears silently turned their heads to follow the flight of the ball. Buttermaker rose slowly to his feet, as did the fans in the stands.

Then everyone was motionless, except Timmy Lupus. He backed up and backed up and backed up, finally bumping into the fence. He held his glove up, over the top of the fence, and closed his eyes. The ball plopped into his glove.

A shocked silence was followed by riotous cheering.

The stands roared with praise, as did all the Bears. Mrs. Lupus dabbed her eyes with a handkerchief. The only quiet one then was Timmy. He still held his glove above the fence, with his eyes closed. Slowly he opened them and brought down his glove. He stared into it, at the ball. A smile sprang to his face, and tears dribbled down into his mouth.

The entire team raced into right field, Tanner leading. They hoisted Timmy up above their shoulders, with him still holding the ball in his glove, and danced with him all the way to the dugout.

"LUPUS!" Tanner bellowed merrily, "you fantastic, nose-picking CRUD, you! The most fantastic catch I EVER SEEN!"

Several fans raced down and surrounded the elevated Timmy. Even Cool Carl Karansky appeared and reached up to slap his back.

Then, as quickly as it had begun, the cheering and tumult stopped. The Bears had one last chance at the plate. They were trailing, 7–3.

The Bears sat in the dugout, breathing heavily. "We need five runs," Ahmad said, straining to get his wind, "BAD."

"Darn right," Tanner said. "Gimme a cruddy bat."

The team rose to bark encouragement as Tanner went to the plate.

"Pound one good, man!" "Get her started!" "Bat around, Bears, everybody hits!"

Tanner lunged at the first pitch and hit it on the ground between third and short, into left field. He reached first but had no intention of stopping there. Head down, he rounded the bag and dug for second.

"NO, TANNER!" Buttermaker covered his eyes.

Tanner dove head-first for the bag as the second-baseman took and threw and slapped on the tag.

A moan went up from the bench as the umpire raised his thumb for the out.

"WHAT'S THE MATTER WITH YOU, UMP?" Tanner screeched as he sprang to his feet, fists clenched. "I was safe by a YEAR! I oughta—"

Buttermaker grabbed Tanner away as the umpire shook his head and folded his arms regally.

"I was SAFE, Coach!" Tanner said, kicking the dirt savagely.

"YOU BET!" Buttermaker said. "Hey, ump, you're BLIND!" He hauled Tanner back to the dugout.

Engelberg stepped in. He fouled off the first pitch. The Bears pressed forward out of the dugout, clapping.

"Wait for a GOOD ONE, babe!" Buttermaker called.

"WE'RE NOT OUT OF THIS ONE YET!" Tanner screamed.

Engelberg hit a ground ball to third. He lumbered toward first, his heavy legs churning up dirt, his face contorted with strain, his arms pumping wildly.

"GO, GO, GO!"

The throw beat him by a step.

The Bears sat back, exhausted, nearly finished. Several fans got up to leave. A couple of cars pulled out of the parking lot.

The Bears fought to hold back tears.

Buttermaker stomped his feet and clapped his hands. "COME ON! WE'RE NOT BEATEN! ON YOUR FEET, BEARS!"

They rose dutifully, and began tired cheering and clapping.

"OGILVIE!" Buttermaker barked.

Ogilvie's eyes sprang wide open with terror. "I can't BREATHE, I—"

"You're UP!"

Ogilvie drew himself erect painfully, and walked toward the plate beside Buttermaker.

"You can make it, Ogilvie," Buttermaker said. "This is your chance to help the team." He put his arm around Ogilvie's quivering shoulders. "Hey, what are you so nervous about?"

"Without going into much detail," Ogilvie said, his voice breaking, "I'm 0 for 14 on the year. Next to Timmy, I'm probably the worst player in the history of this league. And, well . . ." He shook spastically. Buttermaker hugged him tight, relaxing him a little. "And, well, the odds of me—"

"Ogilvie." Buttermaker smiled. "To hell with the odds on this one."

"All right," Ogilvie said, gritting his teeth, "perhaps the law of averages will—"

"You're the next batter, Ogilvie, that's all."

"Right, Coach. Here I go."

Buttermaker retreated to the bench and waved his hands to stir the Bears' support.

"Come on, Ogilvie . . ." "BIIIG hitter up there . . ." "Good eye, Ogilvie . . ." "We're all BEHIND ya, babe . . ."

The first pitch was a called strike. Ogilvie danced around on one foot and the other, then stepped back in and bounced up and down in a crouch as if on a spring. The next pitch was called strike two.

"SWING AT A GOOD ONE, OGILVIE!" Buttermaker shouted. "YOU CAN DO IT!"

"You think he can do it?" Engelberg asked Tanner, his eyes pleading.

"NATURALLY, you blimp. He's a BEAR, ain't he?"

Ogilvie, shaking like a leaf, now began to wheeze. He

stumbled back out of the batter's box and fumbled in his pocket for his asthma medication. He took out the little tube, dropped it in the dirt, picked it up, and stuck it to his nose, grit and all, and inhaled deeply.

"This ain't algebra," chuckled the catcher, "IS it, Ogilvie?"

Ogilvie glared at the catcher. His anger quelled his shaking. He stepped back up to the plate.

Joey Turner lobbed one in. Ogilvie swung and fouled it off in the dirt, the first pitch he had touched this season.

"Way to GO, Ogilvie!" "Way to HANG IN!"

Ogilvie bent down to rub some dirt onto his hands. The next pitch was lobbed in. Ogilvie barely held up his swing to take ball one. Then ball two.

Joey kicked the dirt disgustedly around the mound and slapped his glove against his leg.

Ogilvie hopped around nervously, glancing over at the bench for encouragement.

Joey leaned back and fired a fast ball.

Ogilvie, who happened to be blinking, never saw it.

"BALL THREE!" called the umpire.

Another lob. Ogilvie fouled it off in the dirt and fell down.

Then a fast ball, which caught Ogilvie looking at the dugout.

"BALL FOUR!"

Ogilvie scampered toward first base, waving his fists in the air.

"That's my OGILVIE!" bellowed Engelberg.

Buttermaker whispered some instructions to Ahmad and sent him up. Ahmad dug in and growled at the catcher: "Jus' you watch THIS smoker, chump! It's goin' OUTTA here!"

Ahmad laid down a perfect drag bunt halfway up the

third-base line, and easily beat it out, Engelberg advancing to second.

The scattered cheers which greeted Ogilvie's walk now swelled. People began returning to the stands, which became alive with buzzing chatter.

Roy Turner paced in front of the Yankee's dugout. "Everybody stay COOL out there!" he yelled. "We're WAY AHEAD!"

Miguel muttered to himself in Spanish as he set himself and took ball one.

Joey Turner began pitching more impatiently, taking less time to study his catcher's target. Ball two and ball three came past Miguel. The fourth was in the dirt.

The bases were loaded with Bears. Kelly Leak walked casually to the plate.

Everybody in the stands rose to their feet at the dramatic sight of the league's best hitter coming up for potentially the tying run.

The first pitch was way outside; so was the second. They were going to walk him, willing to force in a run to get to the next weak hitter, Lefty Stein.

Buttermaker trotted up to Kelly and whispered in his ear. Kelly nodded.

The crowd hushed. Then suddenly there came a mighty voice bellowing from the stands: "HEY, LEAK! PUT ONE IN THE PACIFIC! LET 'EM KNOW WHO YOU ARE!"

All eyes turned toward the voice. All except Kelly's. He knew it was his father.

The third pitch came in like the first two, a pitchout. But Kelly shifted his stance, lunged out, and smashed the ball down the right-field line.

Ogilvie scored, then Ahmad, then Miguel. Kelly blazed around first, then second, as the right-fielder finally reached the ball.

People poured out of the stands, pressing against the first and third-base lines, screaming cheers and fears.

The right-fielder bobbled the ball, then grabbed it and heaved a mighty throw toward the plate.

Kelly never looked up and never let up as he rounded third. The throw took one hop, two, three, hit the catcher's glove as Kelly went into a desperate slide . . .

"YER . . . OUT!"

The action froze for an instant with the umpire's thumb upraised, Kelly's foot on the plate, the catcher's tag on Kelly's leg.

Then it was over.

A solemn crowd stood around the Bears' dugout, oblivious to the celebration going on around the Yankees across the field. Mr. Tower put his arm around Regi, who, like many, was crying. Mrs. Agilar held out a tissue to her two boys, who shook their heads, refusing it. Ahmad's brothers each had an arm around him. Mrs. Lupus stood silently beside Timmy. Lefty and Engelberg and Ogilvie patted one another's backs mournfully. Tanner, Kelly, and Amanda huddled together, their hands clasped with each other's. Councilman Whitewood stood with his head bowed near Toby and Buttermaker. Just outside the group, Brenda held her head proudly high.

Buttermaker glanced at her, then suddenly broke into a run, heading for his car.

In moments he was back, lugging a cardboard case. He strode into the somber gathering and plopped the case down. He ripped it open.

"ENGELBERG!"

Engelberg looked up, his eyes red. Buttermaker tossed him a can of beer.

Engleberg caught the beer and studied it quizzically. "What's this?"

"We're celebrating, Bears," Buttermaker said, tossing cans to other players.

"BUTTERMAKER!" Councilman Whitewood's eyes appeared ready to explode.

"Why we celebrating?" Ahmad asked meekly.

"Because you should be DARN PROUD of yourselves," Buttermaker said, tossing out the rest of the cans. "Because you were plenty of BAD NEWS for a lot of teams in this league."

Tanner caught his can and held it up. "I'll drink to that," he said, suddenly cheerful.

"Me too," Amanda said, lifting her sore arm out of the ice bucket to hoist a can.

"But, but," Councilman Whitewood sputtered, "these are . . . CHILDREN!"

"Yeah," Buttermaker said, smiling at him. "They taught us adults a lot, didn't they? They deserve champagne, but the pool-cleaning business suffered a bit during the season, so we had to settle for beer." He rose and held a beer can aloft. "I propose a toast!"

All the Bears held up their beers.

"To the BEST DARN BUNCH OF BALLPLAYERS EVER TO WEAR BEARS' UNIFORMS!"

They laughed and cheered and tipped the cans to their lips. Even Councilman Whitewood tapped his can against Toby's and drank.

"Buttermaker?"

Roy Turner stood outside the bunch, his Yankee team behind him.

"Yeah, Coach?" Buttermaker said.

"Buttermaker, my boys got something they want to say."

The Bears stared at them. The Yankees nervously shuffled their feet. Several of them spoke, their voices blending together:

"We just want to say . . ." "you played a good game . . . we treated you guys pretty bad all season . . ." "and we want to apologize for the . . . we think you're a pretty good team . . . not all THAT good, but . . . but a pretty good team . . . and with a whole lot of GUTS . . . yeah, guts, and HEART . . . so, congratulations . . . from us Yankees."

Turner faced his team and led them in the cheer: "Two, four, six, eight—who do we appreciate? BEARS! BEARS! BEARS!" They tossed their caps into the air, picked them up, and headed back for their own dugout.

"YANKEES!" Timmy Lupus took a step toward them. Everyone stopped and looked back. "HEY, YANKEES!" Even the Bears were dumfounded. Then Timmy began to stammer. "I just want to say, uh, er, what I . . . I just . . ." He glanced at Buttermaker. "Oh, HECK! I just want to say that you can take your apology . . . AND STUFF IT IN YOUR EAR!"

The Bears stood, shocked, then smiled, then erupted in a pandemonic cheer, leaping up and down with fists waving.

Timmy took another step toward the stunned Yankees. "JUST WAIT TILL NEXT YEAR!"

Timmy turned and marched back to the screaming, dancing mass of Bears with a kingly stride. They pulled him into their midst, slapping him on the back, shoulders, head.

Councilman Whitewood leaned in to Buttermaker's ear, to be heard over the din. "Can I believe that's Timmy LUPUS?"

"Of course!" Buttermaker said, shoving him aside and plunging into the happy, struggling crush of Bears. "Nobody messes with Timmy Lupus—or any of us Bears!"

The story behind Bobbie Gentry's legendary song

In Tallahatchie County, Mississippi, people still talk about the dusty June day in 1953 when for no apparent reason Billy Joe McAllister jumped off the Tallahatchie Bridge.

Now, years after the whispers and rumors, the muddy Tallahatchie River gives up its secrets——the secrets within the haunting ballad that swept America. And bestselling author Herman Raucher writes a love story that is beautiful, tender, funny, joyous and ultimately so heart-breaking that you will never forget it.

Soon to be a Max Baer/Warner Bros. film

by the author of *Summer of '42*

HERMAN RAUCHER'S
Ode To Billy Joe

DECEMBER 11, 1944 ... U.S.S. *Candlefish*, submarine on wartime patrol, mysteriously lost at Latitude 30 in the Pacific. All hands perish, except for one survivor.

OCTOBER 5, 1974 ... Six hundred miles northwest of Pearl Harbor, a submarine surfaces in front of a Japanese freighter. It is the *Candlefish*, in perfect working order fully outfitted down to steaks in the freezer yet without a trace of life aboard.

In Washington, D.C., a naval intelligence officer is convinced that the *Candlefish* was the victim of another Devil's Triangle, and convinces his superiors to send it on a voyage retracing her route of thirty years before in the hope of uncovering whatever fearful force lies in wait at Latitude 30.

Only when the sub is well out to sea, with no turning back, do he and the rest of the crew begin to suspect why the *Candlefish* has come back from a watery grave, and what that means to every living soul aboard.

GHOSTBOAT

by George E. Simpson and Neal R. Burger

BESTSELLERS FROM DELL

fiction

☐ RICH MAN, POOR MAN by Irwin Shaw $1.95 (7424-29)
☐ GHOSTBOAT
   by George Simpson and Neal Burger $1.95 (5421-00)
☐ ODE TO BILLY JOE by Herman Raucher $1.75 (6628-17)
☐ WHERE ARE THE CHILDREN? by Mary H. Clark $1.95 (9593-04)
☐ THE FORTY-FIRST THIEF
   by Edward A. Pollitz, Jr. $1.75 (5420-01)
☐ CRY MACHO by N. Richard Nash $1.95 (4915-06)
☐ THE OTHER SIDE OF MIDNIGHT
   by Sidney Sheldon $1.75 (6067-07)
☐ MARATHON MAN by William Goldman..... $1.95 (5502-02)
☐ HERS by A. Alvarez $1.75 (5052-06)
☐ MRS. 'ARRIS GOES TO MOSCOW
   by Paul Gallico $1.50 (5713-07)

non-fiction

☐ BREACH OF FAITH by Theodore H. White ... $1.95 (0780-14)
☐ GREEN BEACH by James Leasor $1.95 (4491-03)
☐ HOLLYWOOD BABYLON by Kenneth Anger .. $5.95 (5325-07)
☐ DR. SIEGAL'S NATURAL FIBER PERMANENT
   WEIGHT LOSS DIET
   by Sanford Siegal, D.O., M.D. $1.75 (7790-25)
☐ THE LAST TESTAMENT OF LUCKY LUCIANO
   by Martin A. Gosch and Richard Hammar ... $1.95 (4940-21)
☐ THE ULTRA SECRET by F. W. Winterbotham .. $1.95 (9061-07)
☐ MEETING AT POTSDAM by Charles L. Mee, Jr. $1.95 (5449-08)
☐ EST: Playing the Game the New Way
   by Carl Frederick $3.95 (2365-13)
☐ WAMPETERS, FOMA & GRANFALLOONS
   by Kurt Vonnegut, Jr. $1.95 (8533-25)
☐ THE NEW ASSERTIVE WOMAN
   by L.Z. Bloom, K. Coburn and J. Pearlman .. $1.75 (6393-10)

Buy them at your local bookstore or use this handy coupon for ordering:

Dell | **DELL BOOKS**
P.O. BOX 1000, PINEBROOK, N.J. 07058

Please send me the books I have checked above. I am enclosing $_____
(please add 35¢ per copy to cover postage and handling). Send check or money
order—no cash or C.O.D.'s. Please allow up to 8 weeks for shipment.

Mr/Mrs/Miss_____

Address_____

City_____State/Zip_____